"I had planned on an early night but couldn't put this book down until I finished it around 3am. Like her other books, this one features fascinating characters with a plot that mimics real life in the best way. My recommendation: it's time to read every book Tammy L Grace has written."
— *Carolyn, review of Beach Haven*

"This book is a clean, simple romance with a background story very similar to the works of Debbie Macomber. If you like Macomber's books you will like this one. A holiday tale filled with dogs, holiday fun, and the joy of giving will warm your heart."
— *Avid Mystery Reader, review of A Season for Hope: A Christmas Novella*

"This book was just as enchanting as the others. Hardships with the love of a special group of friends. I recommend the series as a must read. I loved every exciting moment. A new author for me. She's fabulous."
—*Maggie!, review of Pieces of Home: A Hometown Harbor Novel (Book 4)*

"Tammy is an amazing author, she reminds me of Debbie Macomber… Delightful, heartwarming…just down to earth."
— *Plee, review of A Promise of Home: A Hometown Harbor Novel (Book 3)*

"This was an entertaining and relaxing novel. Tammy Grace has a simple yet compelling way of drawing the reader into the lives of her characters. It was a pleasure to read a story that didn't rely on theatrical tricks, unrealistic events or steamy sex scenes to fill up the pages. Her characters and plot were strong enough to hold the reader's interest."
—*MrsQ125, review of Finding Home: A Hometown Harbor Novel (Book 1)*

"This is a beautifully written story of loss, grief, forgiveness and healing. I believe anyone could relate to the situations and feelings represented here. This is a read that will stay with you long after you've completed the book."
—*Cassidy Hop, review of Finally Home: A Hometown Harbor Novel (Book 5)*

"Killer Music is a clever and well-crafted whodunit. The vivid and colorful characters shine as the author gradually reveals their hidden secrets—an absorbing page-turning read."
— *Jason Deas, bestselling author of Pushed and Birdsongs*

"I could not put this book down! It was so well written & a suspenseful read! This is definitely a 5-star story! I'm hoping there will be a sequel!"
—*Colleen, review of Killer Music*

"This is the best book yet by this author. The plot was well crafted with an unanticipated ending. I like to try to leap ahead and see if I can accurately guess the outcome. I was able to predict some of the plot but not the actual details which made reading the last several chapters quite engrossing."

—*0001PW, review of Deadly Connection*

UNCHARTED WATERS

UNCHARTED WATERS

SAIL AWAY SERIES BOOK 3

TAMMY L. GRACE

LONE MOUNTAIN PRESS

Uncharted Waters
A Standalone Novel
Tammy L. Grace

UNCHARTED WATERS is a work of fiction. Names, characters, places, and incidents either are products of the author's imagination or are used fictitiously. Any resemblance to actual events, locales, entities, or persons, living or dead, is entirely coincidental.

UNCHARTED WATERS Copyright © 2023 by Tammy L. Grace

All rights reserved. No part of this book may be reproduced or transmitted in any form or by any means, electronic or mechanical including photocopying, recording, or by any information storage and retrieval system without the written permission of the author, except for the use of brief quotations in a book review. For permissions contact the author directly via electronic mail: tammy@tammylgrace.com

www.tammylgrace.com
Facebook: https://www.facebook.com/tammylgrace.books
Twitter: @TammyLGrace
Instagram: @authortammylgrace
Published in the United States by Lone Mountain Press, Nevada

ISBN (eBook) 978-1-945591-32-7
ISBN (Print) 978-1-945591-39-6
FIRST EDITION
Printed in the United States of America
Cover Design by Elizabeth Mackey Graphic Design

ALSO BY TAMMY L. GRACE

COOPER HARRINGTON DETECTIVE NOVELS

Killer Music

Deadly Connection

Dead Wrong

Cold Killer

HOMETOWN HARBOR SERIES

Hometown Harbor: The Beginning (Prequel Novella)

Finding Home

Home Blooms

A Promise of Home

Pieces of Home

Finally Home

Forever Home

CHRISTMAS STORIES

A Season for Hope: Christmas in Silver Falls Book 1

The Magic of the Season: Christmas in Silver Falls Book 2

Christmas in Snow Valley: A Hometown Christmas Book 1

One Unforgettable Christmas: A Hometown Christmas Book 2

Christmas Wishes: Souls Sisters at Cedar Mountain Lodge

Christmas Surprises: Soul Sisters at Cedar Mountain Lodge

Christmas Shelter: Soul Sisters at Cedar Mountain Lodge

GLASS BEACH COTTAGE SERIES

Beach Haven

Moonlight Beach

Beach Dreams

WRITING AS CASEY WILSON

A Dog's Hope

A Dog's Chance

WISHING TREE SERIES

The Wishing Tree

Wish Again

Overdue Wishes

SISTERS OF THE HEART SERIES

Greetings from Lavender Valley

Remember to subscribe to Tammy's exclusive group of readers for your gift, only available to readers on her mailing list. **Sign up at www.tammylgrace.com. Follow this link to subscribe at https://wp.me/P9umIy-e** and you'll receive the exclusive interview she did with all the canine characters in her Hometown Harbor Series.

Follow Tammy on Facebook by liking her page. You may also follow Tammy on her pages on book retailers or at BookBub by clicking on the follow button.

"The danger of venturing into uncharted waters is not nearly as dangerous as staying on the shore, waiting for your boat to come in."
—Charles F. Glassman

PROLOGUE

It was the last day of school, and the students raced from the building after a busy and shortened day. Now, the halls of Lake Park Elementary were quiet and empty except for bits of paper and forgotten lunchboxes and backpacks.

Jessica toted the last box from her classroom to her car, which she had pulled up to the closest exit. She had already taken most everything home but waited until the last minute to box up the few items that remained on her desk, including the wooden desk plate with MRS. CLARK carved in it that she had used all these years. Despite having been divorced for the last twelve years, she never wanted to confuse her students, so she didn't bother changing her name.

She shut the door of her car. Thirty-two years' worth of supplies and decorations, thirty-two years' worth of memories, all packed safely away in boxes and plastic bins now stacked in her garage.

She took one last look at Room 19 and searched the bare walls and bookshelves for anything she may have left behind. The only things that remained were the colorful, but faded, papers that covered her bulletin boards and the textbooks all neatly stacked in rows on the bookshelves. Her file cabinets stood empty of all the many lessons she had prepared. Without all of her decorations and personal touches, the room was barren and dull. She flicked off the lights and whispered, "Goodbye," while holding back tears that threatened to flow.

She should be happy to be retiring and looking forward to her newfound freedom, but this last year had been one filled with change.

Too many changes.

With each new shift, a little piece of her broke off and floated away. Teaching had been her life, her only career. With the end of the school year always a rush, Jessica hadn't had much time to dedicate to figuring out how she would fill her days. She knew she could make it through the next few months, since she could pretend it was just like any other summer break, but what would she do when fall came? She vowed not to think about it right now and steeled herself for the last hours she would spend at the brick building she had called home for so long.

She made her way to the multi-purpose room, where the end-of-year parties were always held. She was the only teacher retiring this year, which made it impossible to escape being the center of attention. As usual, there was a huge buffet of homemade food, and Jessica filled a plate, only to be polite and have something to do. Her stomach was doing flips, and she wasn't sure she could eat much.

Jessica's throat tightened as she listened to Principal Reynolds review her history as an educator on Mercer Island. He started with her hire date, fresh out of the University of Washington. He went through the litany of elementary schools where she had taught and ended with her last seventeen years spent in Room 19 of Lake Park Elementary, as a beloved fifth-grade teacher. He hinted, not too subtly, that he expected to see her back as a substitute teacher in the fall.

Everyone clapped when he ended his tribute and presented Jessica with a bouquet of flowers and a pin commemorating her years of service. Mrs. Tanner, a third-grade teacher who took care of all the social committee activities for the staff, rushed over to Jessica's side before she could escape back to the plate of food she had been picking at for the last hour.

Jessica did her best to breathe in and out, hoping with everything she had to quell what felt like the beginning of a panic attack. Experience had taught her breathing was key.

Joleen Tanner had a booming voice and a personality to match. She slung her arm around Jessica's shoulders. "We're all going to miss you so much, Jess. Your quiet kindness and wisdom, your early morning chats over tea in the teachers' lounge, your homemade cookies, and the Christmas play you put on every year. We'll miss all of that, but we'll mostly miss you. We know these last few years haven't been easy ones, and we know how much you miss your mom."

All the teachers' heads bobbed in agreement, as they smiled at Jess. Most of them with the same pity smile they had used when they came to her mother's funeral a few months ago. Her mind drifted back to that horrible day as Joleen droned on.

Her mom's death hadn't been a surprise. It had been years in the making, but it still broke Jess' heart into a million pieces. Her mom had been a huge part of her life and her roommate for twelve years. Ever since Jess divorced, her mother had been her rock. Then when she became ill, their roles reversed, and Jess cared for her, until February, when her frail body finally succumbed.

Everything that had been Jess' normal was slowly disappearing. Years ago, her marriage dissolved in the most horrible way. Then her mom, and now, her lifelong vocation. Her son Jake was grown and living on his own across the country, having elected to be closer to his dad, who lived in Maine, near his family.

Jess always put on a brave face and said it didn't bother her that Jake had chosen Bruce in the divorce, but deep down, it made her heart ache. She could have sullied Bruce in Jake's eyes, but she chose not to do that. She had seen the results of parents who used their children as pawns in a divorce, and she didn't want any part of that.

She'd thought she'd been a good mother and knew Jake loved her, but the sting of rejection hurt. She did her best not to think about it, always working on projects for her classroom or keeping busy in her flower garden, but now, what would she do with all the free time she would have?

Maybe she could convince Jake to come out west to visit, or maybe she could meet him halfway. What was halfway between Seattle and Maine? Minnesota? She was jarred from her thoughts when Joleen thrust a gift bag in front of her.

Joleen's eyes were wide with anticipation as she took hold of the flowers and urged Jess to open the gift, reminding her everyone at the school had chipped in for a special present. Jess smiled and unearthed a shiny folder from the cocoon of tissue paper.

She frowned when she opened it and saw the slick brochures advertising an Alaskan cruise on the *Majestic Star*. Her eyes scanned the information and stopped when she saw the itinerary for a seven-day cruise that left from Seattle in a few weeks.

She wasn't sure if her heart would stop or catapult into her throat.

Breathe.

In and out. In and out.

She'd never been on a cruise. She didn't want to go on a cruise.

Before her mom had gotten ill, she had suggested the two of them take a mother-daughter trip and wanted to try a cruise, but it never happened. Jess pasted a happy smile on her face and was soon engulfed in a tight hug from Joleen.

"Aren't you excited?" she asked, wrapping her arm around Jess. "We all thought after the sacrifices you made taking care of your sweet mom for these last years and working all the time, you deserved an adventure. We're always saying you need to get back out there, and now you'll have the chance."

The walls started to close in, and the breathing wasn't working. Jess stepped away from Joleen, longing for some space and fresh air. Soon, everyone she had worked with made their way to her, shaking her hand or hugging her and congratulating her. All of them were overjoyed at the gift they had contributed to, and Jess played along, hoping she seemed suitably excited.

The thoughtfulness was beyond touching, and that's what she reminded herself each time she thanked one of her colleagues. She didn't know much about cruises, but it filled her heart to know they had gone all out and booked a high-end mini-suite and all the amenities to make sure she had the time of her life.

If only she wanted to go. The thought made her nauseous. What if she got seasick? Or had a panic attack? She would end up spending a week in agony. What about Ruby? She couldn't leave her beloved golden retriever behind. That dog had gotten her through the death of her mom. If not for Ruby, Jess wasn't sure she would have survived the whole ordeal.

Relieved that she had a good excuse not to go, she relaxed and took another deep breath.

After thanking the teachers who lingered behind visiting, she made her way to her car, anxious to get home and spend the evening on the patio with Ruby, as she did each night.

She drove home in under five minutes and pulled into her garage. She loved that about living on Mercer Island. Despite the growth and traffic, she was close to her school and could walk to work most days.

She unloaded the last tote and stacked it with the others. She didn't have the energy to deal with the contents. She collected the gift bag and flowers, along with her purse, and unlocked the door into the house.

Ruby's sweet face was waiting behind it, her

impressive tail wagging from side to side. Her faithful friend waited for Jess each day, in the same spot at the bottom of the stairs. Jess was convinced Ruby could tell time.

They trudged up the stairs from the basement of the tri-level home. With each step, her knees twinged and ached from the extra pounds she had put on over the last few months. Jess tossed her purse on the counter and found a vase for the flowers. Ruby watched her every move, anxious for them to get to their ritual of going out on the patio to relax after work.

Jess poured herself a glass of wine and opened the sliding door off the kitchen. Ruby wriggled through the opening, darted off the patio and onto the grass where she slid across it on her side and then rolled onto her back. Jess took a sip from her glass and vowed to stop the habit she had gotten into after losing her mom. Some of her extra pounds were sure to be from too many bottles of Chardonnay.

Jess opened the Majestic Seas Cruises folder and settled into her favorite chair, propping her feet on the ottoman, while she read through the information again.

She had to admit, the photos of the scenic coastline and gigantic glaciers were stunning. She kept reading and was amazed at the offerings on the ship. It had everything.

She expected pools and hot tubs, shopping, and lots of restaurants, but a movie theatre, a library and art gallery, live music, Broadway shows, lectures and classes, a spa, and several lounges with a variety of music and performances seemed over the top. The dining options alone were overwhelming. She lost count after reading through the descriptions of seven different restaurants. It sounded like something her mom would have loved. Tears burned in her throat as she thought of her mom and what she had missed. If she were still here, they could have gone together.

The brochure made it look awesome, but in the back of her mind, she pictured herself stuck in her cabin, no bigger than a postage stamp, nauseated, and claustrophobic, struggling to breathe.

Alone.

She'd read about those cruises where everyone got sick with some awful stomach flu or when they broke down and were stuck out in the ocean for days. She shook her head and stuck the brochure back in the pocket of the folder. That's when she saw a pink envelope.

She opened it up and found a note from Joleen letting her know she understood it would be hard for Jess to leave Ruby behind and that she had arranged for Jessica's neighbor, Carly, who often watched over Ruby if Jess needed to be away, to housesit and take care of Ruby for the week.

Carly was a responsible teenager, who would be a senior next year and in addition to Ruby loving her, Jess trusted her. Not to mention Carly's parents were caring and responsible and right next door should she need help.

She sighed. "That darn Joleen thought of everything."

Jess rested her head against the back of the chair, willing herself to concentrate on the colorful flowers she loved that graced the pots along the patio and the beds she kept tended near the edge of the grass.

This was her oasis.

Her happy spot.

Her safe zone.

The idea of getting on a ship with thousands of other people, all of them strangers, and floating around the ocean for a week was not how she wanted to spend her first taste of freedom. But how could she refuse to go after all the money her colleagues had spent and all the work she knew Joleen put into the gift?

She shuddered to think what it had cost. Jess would have rather had the amount they spent on a gift card at the garden center or the bookstore. She shook her head. Now, she just sounded like a spoiled brat or a curmudgeon. Joleen and the others had her best interest at heart, and they had been hounding her for a few months that she needed to start living again.

They assumed caring for her mom had been a burden.

They didn't understand it was a privilege.

Jess had spent much of her life doing what made others happy. As she thumbed through the brochure again, she realized this cruise would be no different. There was no way she could decline the trip; all it would do if she brought it up was make for hard feelings with the people who were the closest thing to friends she had.

She finished her wine and went inside to grab a notepad and her tablet. If she couldn't get out of it, she better get prepared with all the anti-nausea paraphernalia and medication available. She'd have to practice all her tricks to keep her panic attacks under control.

The brochure had a handy section for first-time cruisers and a suggested list of what to pack. She perused both and started jotting down a list.

She only had a few weeks before she'd be stepping aboard the *Majestic Star* and setting sail for what the brochure and the photos of the smiling crew promised to be a restful and enjoyable week, filled with pampering, fine dining, and jaw-dropping scenery.

Jess hoped the knot in her stomach was senseless nerves and not a portend of what could be a long and miserable seven days.

ONE

It was a perfect summer day in Seattle. The sun was shining above the beautiful waters as Jess wheeled her suitcase to the pier. The ship was due to sail at four o'clock, but passengers were permitted to board at noon. Jess had already attached her *Majestic Star* luggage tags to her bag and had her carry-on ready. Joleen suggested Jess be at the pier at eleven o'clock, explaining it was best to be early so she could get on board and explore the ship.

At the terminal, the friendly porters with red caps helped travelers, and one of them took her bag for her. She stepped into the line of passengers waiting to go through the boarding process and embark. Her friends who had been on cruises before assured Jess her cabin was in a great part of the ship. It was on the Aloha Deck or Deck 12 of the *Majestic Star* and close to the middle of the ship, which promised a smooth ride.

The long line moved swiftly as happy chatter filled the air, with the mood of the passengers high and excited to board. Jess hoped some of that enthusiasm would rub off on her. Her stomach was tied in knots, and she longed to get onto the ship and locate her cabin.

As she surveyed the lines, she noticed lots of families, older couples, young couples with their arms wrapped around each other, and several groups of women, all waiting to board. Her heart sank when she realized she was the only single traveler in the throng of people in her immediate area. The idea of sticking out like a sore thumb didn't appeal to Jess, and she hoped she could disappear so nobody would notice she was alone.

Minutes later, she was at the front of the line and after a warm welcome and a quick scan of the special cruise bracelet she had received in the mail, that would be her electronic key to unlocking her room and other amenities, she followed the directions to the security checkpoint. After the scan, she continued to one of the colorful tents outside the small gangways that stretched from the pier to the interior of the ship. She was in the turquoise-blue group and after a few minutes, was welcomed aboard.

Everywhere she looked, crewmembers assisted passengers with directions and before she could ask for help, a young woman in white pants and a deep-blue polo shirt with the Majestic logo greeted her. Veronica, as her nametag displayed, helped Jess get her bearings and pointed out the elevators and stairs that would take her to the other decks.

Jess smiled at the young woman. "I must look like a first-timer, huh?"

She laughed. "You just looked overwhelmed, which is understandable if this is your first trip. We're delighted you chose the *Majestic Star*. It's a fabulous ship and our newest." She reminded Jess that the guest services desk was her go-to place if she needed any help at all. "We're on Deck 5 now, so if you lose your bearings or need help figuring something out, just return to Deck 5, and someone on the crew will be happy to help you. Chances are you'll run into a crewmember before you even make it back here. You can ask anyone with a nametag like mine, and they'll help you or get you to the right place for what you need."

Veronica gestured to the area beyond the service desk. "That's our spa and if you want to book a treatment, it's a great time to get that done. They fill up quickly." She turned and directed Jess' attention to the other side. "This is our Grand Atrium, and it's always a hub of activity." Jess nodded as she took in the elegant space that reminded her of old town squares in European cities. The open space was ringed by cafes and shops and at its centerpiece was a gorgeous double spiral staircase with glass elevators in the midst. As she looked up, she noticed the huge chandeliers and beautiful glass sculptures that hung in the space.

Using a colorful map, Veronica pointed out the pools on the Lido deck and also directed Jess' attention to the main dining room and some of the specialty restaurants. "Tonight, all the specialty restaurants offer guests a discount, so if you're interested in trying one, now's the time to make a reservation."

"This is even more impressive in person than in the brochure photos," said Jess, as she gawked above her, watching people on the stairs and in the elevators.

"The only thing you need to remember is to report to your muster station for the safety drill, and that usually happens about an hour before we sail. There's also a sailing party on the upper decks. They'll have music and dancing, and it's one big celebration."

Jess' heart beat faster. Veronica added, "Get there early and grab a spot away from the bandstand. There are places on both the Lido and Sun deck near the aft of the ship that will give you a great view and will be a bit quieter and less crowded. That's Deck 16 and 17. Since it's your first cruise, you'll have to grab a spot at the railing and wave as you sail away."

Jess couldn't help but relax as the cheerful young woman explained things and gave her some insider tips. She handed her a flyer and let her know they were hosting a Murder Mystery Game tonight in the theatre. Maybe this wouldn't be so bad after all. She thanked her and set off to book the spa treatments that her colleagues had so thoughtfully included and made a reservation for dinner at a French restaurant on the Promenade Deck that caught her eye.

With that out of the way, she took the stairs, at a leisurely pace, to the Aloha Deck, five decks above, to find her cabin. She had managed to lose four measly pounds since school adjourned and hoped to get in some exercise while on the cruise. She used her bracelet to open the door and stepped inside the mini suite. She noticed the two sets of heavy curtains, reminding her of the long bouts of daylight she would experience on the excursion. One set could be drawn between the bedroom area and the sitting area with the couch and television next to it. The other set could be closed across the balcony.

Her luggage wasn't in her room, which wasn't a surprise. She put down her carry-on bag. She had chosen to bring her mom's well-used leather backpack, which would be useful on the excursions she'd be taking. She ran her hands over the soft leather. Having it close would make it seem like a part of her mom was on the cruise with her.

She stepped across the space to investigate the bathroom, which was small but serviceable, and then opened the balcony doors. Her cabin was situated so that it had a larger balcony with an angled extension. She took a deep breath and sat in one of the outdoor chairs. The view was lovely, as was the fresh air.

She never would have survived an inside cabin.

Sitting here, sipping tea and reading a book, might be close to perfection. Thinking about a latte made her stomach growl. She wasn't sure she was ready to tackle the buffet, but there were plenty of other quick options for a bite to eat.

She went back inside and found the schedule of activities on the desk, reminding her to watch the safety video and report to her muster station when the drill was announced. She checked the information to find the location where she was to report on Deck 7 and found the life vest in the closet.

She stowed most of her carry-on items and after a swipe of lip gloss, she took her handbag and headed to find a latte and something to eat. She settled on the café back on Deck 5 with the sinful-looking pastries. Along with a chocolate croissant she couldn't resist, and a latte, she selected a cup of fresh fruit.

The crowd roaming the Grand Atrium had grown since her arrival. She took her food and headed up the stairs, hoping to find a spot to sit outside and enjoy the fresh air. She found a deck chair and small table available on the Promenade Deck and settled in, doing a bit of people watching while she enjoyed the buttery pastry and the warm latte. Once she was done, she didn't linger long. She knew the muster drill would be happening soon and didn't want to fight a crowd to get back to her cabin and then down to the deck. She cleaned up her table, took what was left of the latte with her, and found the stairway.

She had just dug out her tablet so she could get the Wi-Fi set up on it, when there was a knock on her cabin door. She opened it and found a smiling woman with her shiny hair pulled into a ponytail, dressed in a black uniform with a white apron. "I'm your cabin stewardess, Mariah. Please let me know if you need anything at all." She pointed at the card on the desk with her name.

Mariah checked to make sure Jess understood where to go for the muster drill and promised her luggage would be placed in her room as soon as possible, but no later than after dinner. Jess thanked her and went back to her tablet, which she got connected and then scrolled to a book she hoped to finish.

As she sat on the balcony reading, her eyes got heavier and heavier. She was roused from her sleepy state by the sound of horns and an announcement for the muster drill. She hurried to grab her life vest and headed for the stairs. Her heart thudded as she descended the stairs. The idea of an emergency at sea was one of the reasons she wasn't thrilled to be on a cruise. She had seen *Titanic* too many times.

The process was organized with the crew stationed to help passengers to their designated locations. The safety video was available for those who had not yet watched it, and experts were on hand to help those who didn't know how to put on a life vest. Jess resisted the urge that came from too many years of teaching, to shush the passengers that were complaining and moaning about the waste of time.

Some might view it as a waste, but like the hundreds of fire drills she had been through at school, Jess knew how important it was to know what to do in the face of an emergency. Being new to cruising and hesitant, she paid close attention to all the advice and committed to memory the path she would take to Deck 7.

After scanning her bracelet and having a crew member check her life vest, she was free to go. She made a quick detour to pick up some bottled water to keep in the small refrigerator in her room and couldn't resist a couple of bottles of iced tea.

She trekked back to her cabin, toting her shopping bag and her life jacket and then, taking Veronica's advice to heart, headed to the stairs and the upper decks for her first sailing experience.

She made a quick decision and set out for the Sun Deck, taking the stairway nearest the aft of the ship. By the time she reached the door for the deck, her legs were burning, and her knees were complaining. She would earn her French dinner and whatever decadent dessert she wanted tonight.

The music was booming from the speakers when she opened the door and searched for an open spot along the railing. She found some empty space on the port side, leaned against it while she took in the view of Seattle, and noticed the infinity-style pool. She took note, hoping it would be a quieter spot to enjoy a dip than the larger pools in the middle of the deck.

Photos taken of passengers when they boarded flashed on the huge screen that hovered over the deck and pools. Jess was even happier she had declined the offer from the photographer. The last thing she needed was her face on the big screen, advertising she was alone. How pathetic would that look?

Captain Wyman popped up on the screen to welcome the passengers aboard, promising smooth sailing and a trip of a lifetime. Along with the captain, other leadership of the ship were introduced and delivered welcoming messages.

The band played a variety of hits from decades gone by, and the passengers were getting into the spirit, dancing and singing along. Even Jess tapped her toes to their rendition of "I Love Rock 'n Roll" while she watched the big screen, waiting for the countdown to sail. Crew members and dancers led passengers in forming groups to dance together or in long lines that snaked through the deck.

After that song ended, a familiar tune she recognized came from the speakers and after a few moments and a visual cue from the screen, she recognized the theme from *The Love Boat* and smiled as a recording from the original television crew flashed on the screen. Captain Stubing and some of the other actors, from what had to be decades ago, welcomed the guests aboard and promised them a cruise to remember.

The emcee returned to the stage and got the crowd revved up, counting down from ten, and then the loud horns of the ship sounded as they pulled away from the pier. The skyline view of Seattle was nothing short of magnificent, and Jess was glad Veronica encouraged her to take advantage of experiencing the scene, watching the people on the dock wave and wish the passengers well.

It reminded her of one of her favorite Cary Grant movies, *An Affair to Remember*. Scenes from the film trickled through her mind. Sailing in the 50s was much different than today. She recalled the tuxedos and gowns in the movie. Looking around the deck, it was clear the days of dressing up for sailing were over.

She stayed on deck and watched the landmarks she recognized fade away as the ship set out to the vast expanse of the Pacific to make her way to the first stop in Juneau. Jess knew they would spend the rest of today and tomorrow at sea. The idea of being in the open water shifted her mind to worry, and her imagination bloomed with worst-case scenarios.

Once they got to Juneau, the ship would make her way back down the coast along the inside passage, so land would be visible. The next forty hours would be the worst for Jess. She had to keep her mind occupied.

She wandered downstairs to her cabin and was happy to find her luggage had been delivered. She went about unpacking, hanging her clothes in the closet, and organizing things.

Jess shoved her red rain boots into the closet and placed the wide-brimmed blue sun hat she hoped to use on the top shelf. With only the one formal dining night, she had packed mostly casual clothes. The shimmery jacket she held would have to suffice and looked fancy paired with her black pants and blouse. When they went cruise shopping, Joleen tried to talk her into a dazzling evening gown, but Jess found the pretty jacket on the sale rack and deemed it perfect. She didn't wear dresses much and didn't want to feel more out of her depth than necessary.

Outside of that purchase and a new cardigan with a waterfall hemline in a plum color she loved, she made do with the clothes she wore on a regular basis. Living in Seattle, she had plenty of waterproof outerwear that would work for Alaska.

When she packed, she hadn't planned on having dinner at the French restaurant, but she changed from her yoga style pants into a pair of dressier slacks, a top, and her new plum sweater. She added a necklace and earrings and wore her fancier sandals with heels she'd planned to wear on formal night.

She checked her face and hair in the bathroom mirror, using the curling iron to freshen her hair a bit. Despite getting it colored only two weeks ago, silvery strands were already making their appearance in her natural chestnut-brown hair. Her stylist had suggested a few highlights, and Jess admired the effect and the way they disguised the gray, giving it a summer-kissed look. She finger-styled the loose waves in her shoulder-length, layered style she had worn for several years.

She smiled at her reflection, assuring herself that she looked nice. She had inherited her mother's flawless skin and hazel eyes.

As she glanced down, her smile faded. She had always carried her weight in the lower half of her body and since her mom had died, she'd been overindulging in all the wrong carbs and way too much wine. She knew they weren't good choices but couldn't overcome the cravings for the comfort foods that were like a balm to her broken heart. She was determined to get rid of the weight and find a happy medium between not eating at all, like she had when her mom had been ill, and now stuffing herself with all the wrong things. A cruise ship with twenty-four-hour access to food was probably not the place to succeed, but it did offer more exercise options.

After a quick touch up and some lipstick, she set out for the French restaurant, double checking the map before she left the cabin. With no lines at the glass elevators, she pressed the button for the Promenade Deck. Most of the passengers were still on the deck, taking advantage of the party atmosphere.

The trip down to Deck 7 in the glass elevator was fun, giving her a glimpse of each of the decks, which housed hundreds of cabins. It stopped at every deck and passengers got on and off, all of them sporting friendly smiles. Jess left the elevator, with a gorgeous view of the Promenade Deck and the top of the Grand Atrium which spanned three decks. She was only a few steps away from the French restaurant and when she walked through the door, a friendly hostess greeted her.

She took Jess to a table by the windows, which afforded her a flawless view of the deep blue waters. Her waiter welcomed her with olives and cheese, along with fresh bread. The restaurant offered a fixed-price menu, and Jess chose from a list of appetizers, entrees, and desserts. She passed on the bread, saving her calories for the dessert, and couldn't resist the free glass of wine the server offered as a welcome aboard gift.

After a delicious filet mignon, preceded by a salmon appetizer, she took her first bite of the chocolate tart. The smooth and rich chocolate custard was heavenly. Her mom would have loved it. They both shared an affinity for all things chocolate.

She savored each morsel, soaking in the ambience of the beautiful décor and the stunning sea view while she enjoyed the dessert with a cup of steaming Earl Grey tea.

After a harried morning and dealing with the unease of being a first-time cruiser, Jess gazed out the window and sighed. She might be able to get used to the ship, relax, and enjoy herself like Joleen had promised.

After lingering as long as she could, she used her special bracelet to add the meal to her bill. It had been worth every penny.

TWO

Following dinner, Jess detoured to the theatre for the Murder Mystery Game. There, the audience was treated to a play of sorts with staff members in costume playing the part of the suspects and one poor soul getting murdered.

The premise was a movie after party, with the director being murdered. It reminded her of the old board game of Clue, with a variety of suspects all decked out in memorable costumes and all with plausible motives and weak alibis. The host explained that passengers could collect clues from various places aboard the ship and interact with the characters on the Promenade Deck each day of the cruise. The characters would reveal more clues throughout the voyage, and the murderer would be divulged the last evening of the cruise.

Jess collected her folder of information that outlined the suspects and the murder and then took a short tour to check out the jogging path on the Sky Deck. After, she detoured to the Lido Deck to scope out the buffet and the glass walkway that arched out over the top of the water to allow a view all the way down to the sea. Jess stood on the deck, just steps away from it, amazed at the engineering, but hesitated to actually walk across the glass floor.

She marveled at the enormity of the ship. It was hard to imagine something over a thousand feet long and a hundred and fifty feet wide, not to mention two hundred feet high being able to float. When she walked by the buffet, she darted in and selected a tea bag and filled a cup with piping-hot water. Snuggling in and reading was her plan for the rest of the evening.

The stairs and her heeled sandals weren't a great match, so she waited for one of the regular elevators to take her down to Deck 12. When she returned to her cabin, she found a cute towel elephant on her bed, fresh ice in the ice bucket, and a couple of chocolate candies atop her pillow. She smiled and slipped off her sandals.

After changing into her pajamas, she opened the balcony doors to test the temperature. It wasn't what she would call warm, but she craved the fresh air. She used a spare blanket and wrapped it around her body, taking her hot tea, the murder game folder, and a book with her, as she snuggled into a chair. Being on the port side, she had a wonderful view of the sun that would be setting in the next hour.

She put aside her book and her booklight to savor the view. She stayed that way, nestled under the blanket, sipping tea, and enjoying the dramatic orb of light dipping into the dark sea. She loved sunsets and over her lifetime, had seen many. This was definitely near the top of the list. There was something special about being in the open water, treated to such wonder. While sensational, it was both idyllic and tranquil.

She gathered her things and locked the door, pulling the heavy drapes across the balcony, content to get under the covers and read until she could sleep. She made a few notes in her murder folder but would need to gather several more clues before she could fathom a guess at the murderer.

As she scanned the pages of her book, she sensed the motion of the ship but tried to distract herself with the story. She turned on the television, hoping the background noise would help divert her temptation to focus on the natural movement of the ship. It worked and soon, she was asleep.

Jess' eyes flew open. Her heart thudded as she took several moments to remember she was on the *Majestic Star*. She had been dreaming, one of those she couldn't remember, but it left her startled and breathless.

She longed for the comfort of Ruby. As much as Jess tried to resist letting the sweet dog sleep on her bed, she couldn't do it. They had been bedmates since the first night Ruby started sleeping outside of her crate. Even then, Jess had positioned her crate right next to her side of the bed so she could reach out and comfort Ruby when she was a puppy and getting acclimated to her forever home.

These days, Ruby was the comforter. Although not trained, Ruby could sense when Jess was about to be afflicted with one of her panic attacks. She'd rush to her side and distract Jess with her snout, push her head under her elbow, and force Jess to focus on her. She'd lick her, circle through her legs, even jump on her to distract her. If she woke from a bad dream, Ruby was right there, snuggling next to her.

Jess longed for the feel of her wet nose against her arm or a quick lick from her big tongue. She hoped Ruby wasn't missing her too much. The darkness and loneliness overwhelmed Jess. After tossing and turning, she threw off the covers and turned on the light. She found her slippers with the outdoor soles and added a jacket over her pajamas that could double as exercise wear. She was glad she left the set with ice-skating penguins home.

She slipped out of the cabin and headed for the Sky Deck and a much-needed walk around the jogging path. It was almost two o'clock in the morning, and the ship was quiet with the passengers tucked into their cabins. When she made it to Deck 18, Jess took a deep breath. From the looks of it, she had the place to herself.

She set out walking the pathway, taking in the massive inky sky filled with twinkling stars. She'd never seen the sky from the open water, and it was amazing. It was hard to tell where the dark water ended, and the open sky began. As she rounded the turn near the aft of the ship, she did a double take.

A beautiful golden retriever hurried to Jess and poked his nose against her hand. It reminded her of how Ruby got her attention. She bent down, confused as to where he came from. Then, she noticed he was wearing a service dog vest. She petted the dog, but he pushed his nose into her hand again and again. She looked around, hoping to see his owner.

The dog trotted away, stopping to look back at Jess until she couldn't resist following him. She jogged after him, and he led her to the other side of the ship, where a man stood next to the railing. Most of his upper body was bent far over it. Jess ran as fast as she could and grabbed the man around his torso.

It was like hugging a massive tree trunk. He moved a bit and shivered, as if startled. He turned his head and straightened his body. Jess still held onto him, unsure of what to do.

Jess looked into his brown eyes, picking up on the alarm she saw in them as she focused on the amber flecks in the dark irises. "Are you okay?" she asked.

The man blinked several times. "Yeah, yeah, I think so. What happened?"

Jess let go of him as he turned and stepped from the railing. "I'm not sure. I came up to take a walk, and your dog pulled me over here. You were sort of hanging over the railing."

He shook his head and reached for the dog. "Good boy, Rebel. Such a good boy." The dog's tail wagged in response and pushed his head into the man's palm, savoring his attention.

Jess glanced down at the beautiful dog and noticed the patch on his vest denoting he was a veteran service dog. She smiled at Rebel. "I have a golden retriever at home and was missing her so much tonight. I had a bad dream." She sighed as Rebel moved even closer to his owner. "May I pet him?"

The man turned his attention to Jess. "I think you've earned that." He smiled and extended his hand to her. "I'm sorry, I'm Dean, and you've met Rebel."

She nodded. "He's magnificent. I'm Jessica. My friends call me Jess." She bent down and ran her hands over the dog's soft ears.

When she stood, Dean searched her face. "I hope you don't think I was going to jump."

Her eyes widened. "Well, I'm not the only one who thought that." She glanced at Rebel and pointed. "He was pretty concerned."

The dog's eyes moved from one to the other as he watched them.

Dean sighed. "I was just feeling really anxious, like a panic attack, and I must have blanked out for a minute. Rebel is trained to get help if he can't snap me out of it, so I'm sure that's why he sought you out."

Jess nodded. "Smart guy." She smiled. "I meant Rebel."

Dean laughed, and some of the strain in his face faded, replaced with a slow smile. "Yeah, I've never been accused of being smart." He patted the dog's side. "Thank you, Jess, if I may call you that, for coming to my rescue."

Her cheeks blossomed as the heat rose from her neck. Suddenly, the jacket felt suffocating. "I didn't do much, but I'm glad I was here. I have some personal experience with panic attacks, so I understand, believe me."

She eyed the man she had rescued, who looked like he would never need help. His wide shoulders and thick arms touted his strength, and she felt it when she had gripped him. He looked like he'd have no trouble wrestling a bear, but there was a gentleness in his eyes that made him vulnerable. She'd always had a soft spot for lost puppies and he reminded her of one.

He gestured to the sports court in the center of the deck, enclosed with netting. "The cruise lets us bring the dogs up here after they close the court. Rebel loves to play ball, so we'd gotten in our hour of fun, and we were heading back when I stopped at the railing. What are you doing out so late?"

She sighed. "I woke up startled from a dream and couldn't go back to sleep. It's my first time on a ship, and I'm uneasy, plus I miss my dog Ruby. She usually sleeps on my bed, and I'm feeling a little lost without her. I didn't want to come on this trip. Did I mention I have panic attacks?" She smiled.

Dean chuckled. "I know that feeling. Rebel here is my rock. I've only had him about a year, but I'd be lost without him." He gestured to the pathway. "We can tag along with you, if you'd like to finish your walk."

"Are you sure you're okay? Do you need to see the doctor or anything?"

He shook his head. "No doctor necessary. I'm feeling better. The panic attacks are a part of my life. I've been doing better, but it's always harder in a new environment."

Dean took hold of Rebel's leash and started walking. With Rebel between them, they made several loops around the deck, taking in the calm evening under the canopy of stars. After a few moments of silence between the two of them, Jess said, "I'm not sure why I told you all that about not wanting to come on the ship. I didn't mean to unload that on you."

Dean held up a hand. "Not to worry. I think I'm the winner in the oversharing competition tonight. I mean it's not every night you tackle a guy you think is going to jump overboard." He stopped and stared at her. "At least I hope you have a better job than that."

She noticed his perfect smile and felt something flutter in her chest. Like his sweet dog, Dean had such expressive and kind eyes. "I just retired from teaching, so I no longer have a job."

"Wow, congratulations. How many years?"

"Thirty-two."

"That's impressive. I'm not sure I could do the same thing for thirty-two years. I bet you were everyone's favorite teacher, right?"

She grinned. "Not sure about that, but it's easy to impress fifth graders. I do run a pretty tight ship, so I'm sure I wasn't everyone's favorite."

His deep laugh filled the deck. "I see what you did there. Already making ship puns."

She smiled and looked out at the water. "I have to admit, I like it more than I thought I would. I'm just not super comfortable on it, but the staff has been fabulous, and all the amenities are wonderful. I'm visiting the spa tomorrow, so we'll see how that goes."

He frowned. "So, that begs the question. Why do you find yourself on a ship, Jess?"

She chuckled. "Great question. It was a gift from my colleagues at work, and I couldn't refuse it without hurting their feelings."

He nodded as they rounded the turn again, keeping up a steady pace with Rebel's tail swishing back and forth in happiness. "Understood. I've been on several ships, but not a pleasure cruise. This is my first one of those. I'm here with a group. It's a veterans group, and several of us have service dogs. They organized the whole thing, and some generous sponsors paid for it. Like you, I felt a bit obligated, and they're great people." He glanced down at

Rebel. "If not for them, I would have never been paired up with this guy."

"He's special, I can tell. My Ruby is also my best friend. She's gotten me through some tough times."

"They are the greatest companions ever. I'm not sure I'd be here without Rebel."

With the gravity of what they each said, Jess couldn't summon any words to add to it, and they made another lap in total silence. After a couple more laps, the first light of day filtered through the clouds.

Jess gasped when she noticed it. "I can't believe it's morning. We've been out here for hours."

"The sun comes up early here. Are you tired?"

She shrugged. "Not really."

"How about I treat you to coffee and breakfast?"

She looked down at her slippers. "Uh, I should probably change my shoes and maybe get dressed. I don't want to scare anyone."

"The buffet isn't open yet, but there's that little café down on Deck 5 that is open twenty-four hours. Shall I meet you there in a few minutes?"

Jess nodded and agreed to it before she even thought about it. They made their way to the elevator, and she got off on Deck 12 while he continued, promising to meet her at the café.

As she walked the hallway to her cabin, she muttered to herself, "I can't believe I agreed to meet a complete stranger for breakfast." In her cabin, she looked in the mirror and shuddered. "Thank goodness I needed to change clothes. My hair is a disaster."

She hurried and changed into her actual exercise clothes she planned to wear for her spa treatments, tamed her hair the best she could, and pinched her cheeks so she didn't look so drab.

She exited the elevators, surprised to see the Grand Atrium almost empty and so quiet. She made her way across the expanse of the open plaza area with the shiny marble-inlaid floor tiles. The shops were closed, as were the bars around the edge of the large courtyard. The café was lit up, and the friendly staff smiled at her from behind the counter, waiting to serve the few passengers who were milling about the ship.

She spotted Dean and Rebel at a cozy table in the corner. As she walked by the long, winding counter, the inviting aroma of coffee tickled her nose. Fresh pastries, sandwiches, and desserts filled the glass cases and made her mouth water.

As she got closer, she was glad she went to her cabin and fixed her hair. The lighting on the deck wasn't great, but now it was hard not to notice Dean's handsome features. His steel-gray hair was trimmed close along both sides and slightly longer on the top. The dark scruff along his chin and cheeks gave him an air of rugged confidence.

When she approached the table, he stood and pulled out her chair. "I hope you haven't been waiting long," she said.

"Just got here. We had to make a quick pit stop for Rebel." He glanced at the counter. "What can I get you?"

"I can't resist their pastries and love croissants, scones, cinnamon rolls. Anything like that and a large chai tea latte would be terrific." She glanced down at her wrist. "Oh, here, take my bracelet. I have the beverage package that includes coffee drinks."

He winked at her and raised the cuff of his jacket to

reveal what looked like a fitness band but included the coin-shaped medallion. "I've got one, too." He gave Rebel the command to stay and set off to the counter.

Rebel's eyes never wandered from Dean. The dog watched as he ordered, waited for the tray, and returned to the table with a selection of pastries and two steaming drinks. Once Dean sat, Rebel relaxed and placed his head on the floor, his eyes closed.

Jess took a sip of her latte and stifled a moan. It was creamy and spicy along with being just the right temperature. Dean took a sip from his cup, and the scent of chocolate wafted from his cup. "Ooh, that smells delicious," she said, taking one of the almond croissants from the tray.

"The barista assured me it's one of their most popular drinks. The chocolate mocha mania." He raised his cup and took another swallow. "It's good." He bit into a bear claw and pronounced it delicious.

"You mentioned a pit stop. Now, I'm curious how they handle service dogs on the ship."

He explained that the steward provided a large box filled with sod that stayed on the balcony. They also supplied bags and a collection can. In addition, they had a similar area, but larger, set up on Deck 10 behind a door for crew access only and in a laundry facility where they washed mops and things. All the handlers with service dogs were permitted to use that area.

She nodded. "Sounds like they have a pretty good system. I never thought about it. It's like an entire city, isn't it? They have everything you could want."

Dean made quick work of his bear claw and moved on to an apple turnover and over the next two hours while they chatted, he talked Jess into splitting a pumpkin scone with him. "I'm going to have to run up and down the stairs to work all of this off," said Jess, as she savored the last bite. "That was delicious though."

"What time is your spa treatment today?" he asked.

"Nine o'clock." She yawned. "I think my second wind is wearing off. I'll probably fall asleep while I'm there."

He grinned. "Yeah, I'm going back to take a nap myself. Maybe we could catch up at dinner. We've got room at our table. We're in the Pearl Dining Room and have an early seating."

"Oh, that would be wonderful. Last night, I ate at the French restaurant since they were offering discounts, so I haven't been to the dining room yet. I can stop by and make sure they change me over to join you."

"Tell them table number thirty-four at five-thirty. I'll introduce you to a few of the people in our group."

"I'd like that. I was dreading how that would work and had a table to myself last night but wasn't looking forward to sitting with strangers tonight." She wrinkled her nose. "I was toying with the idea of ordering room service or having a burger out on the deck."

He laughed. "A woman after my own heart. We'd be happy to have you, and you can meet some of the other service dogs."

At the mention of dogs, Rebel's eyes opened, and his eyebrows rose.

He smiled at his dog. "If things change, just let me know. I'm on the Baja Deck, Cabin 410, and my last name is Nash."

"I better get a move on and get to the spa." She put her

empty plate back on the tray. "Thank you for breakfast, Dean."

He grinned. "It's the least I can do for a woman willing to pull me off the railing." He lowered his voice, "You do realize all the food is free, right?"

She laughed and stood, waving as she made her way out of the café, which was teeming with early morning customers. In fact, she laughed all the way to the spa, where a receptionist smiled and led her to her first treatment of the day.

As she waited on the massage table, the scent of lemon grass in the air, she shut her eyes and smiled. It had been years since she had stayed up all night talking with a man and then shared breakfast with him.

THREE

From the hot stone massage, followed by the luxurious facial with a scalp massage, to the relaxing pedicure and the styling of her hair, Jess enjoyed her hours at the Sea Salt Spa. She was there so long they served her a light lunch and snacks and what seemed like gallons of refreshing citrus-infused water. The spa included a lovely room with a warm and relaxing whirlpool and a cascading rain shower. It was like nothing Jess had ever experienced and quite indulgent.

As she predicted, she fell asleep during the massage. It was the first time since her mom had died that Jess let her mind go blank and focus only on the present instead of worrying about the future or mourning the past. She breathed in the subtle scent of the oil the therapist used and let herself sink into the warm table. She focused on the relaxing aromas and the soft music, not letting her worries seep into mind.

As she left the spa and walked across the Grand Atrium, she noticed the stubborn knot that was usually under her shoulder blade had disappeared. She stopped to get a cup of hot tea and carried it with her. She stood taller, and her footsteps were lighter as she made her way to the stairs, determined to work off a few of the calories she had enjoyed at breakfast.

As she climbed past each deck, she noted the Baja Deck was just one deck below hers. Dean had said Cabin 410, and she was in 414 on her deck. As she traveled the hallway to her cabin, she took note of the numbers and realized 410 was next door to 414, which meant Dean was almost right below her, if the numbers matched up on each deck.

Part of her longed for a nap, but she didn't want to risk ruining her freshly done hair. It was so shiny she took note of the products they used so she could get some when she returned home. She remembered the characters would be on the Promenade Deck, grabbed her murder folder, and took the stairs to Deck 7.

It didn't take long to spot the group, dressed in their lavish costumes, walking along the deck. They stopped every so often and performed as a group, then each of them wandered off alone, where they wrapped a clue in a riddle or short proclamation they shared with the passengers who gathered around them.

She visited each character and made notes in her folder before she took the stairs back to her cabin. Instead of lying on the bed, she opted to spend some time on her balcony and relax with a book and her tea, like she had imagined when she first boarded the ship.

The temperature outside was cooler than it had been yesterday, so she used the blanket cocoon she had perfected last night and was able to finish the book before it was time to get ready for dinner.

Tonight was the formal dining night, so she took extra care with her makeup and didn't have to touch her hair. She added some sparkly drop earrings that picked up on the metallic threads in the jacket she had purchased. The jacket was longer and had the benefit of camouflaging the area below her waist. She rarely dressed up and couldn't remember the last time she had gone anywhere that necessitated it.

After slipping into her heeled sandals again, she made her way to the elevator and set out for the Pearl Dining Room on Deck 6. It was near the aft of the ship, and she hadn't explored it yet. She noted the muted white and beige tones that made up the décor. They, along with the huge waterfall-style crystal chandeliers throughout, gave it an elegant vibe.

She gave her name and the table number Dean had mentioned to the hostess, and she led Jess to a table next to the windows. As Jess passed by several tables, she noticed women wearing fancy beaded gowns, like those Joleen had tried to talk her into, and men in smart tuxedos. She felt a bit underdressed but hated the idea of spending money on a dress she would never wear again.

Dean and Rebel were already seated at the table, as were two other gentlemen. Dean stood, looking quite dashing in his jacket and tie. Jess breathed a sigh of relief when she realized none of them were wearing tuxedos. Dean smiled and introduced her to the other two men seated at the table. Doug and Phil stood and offered her their hands. Both of them had service dogs beside them, one a black Labrador named Ace and the other a golden Labrador named River.

Dean pulled out the chair next to him and waited for Jess to take a seat. She craned her neck to look at the other dogs. "Your dogs are beautiful. I told Dean I was missing my sweet Ruby. She's a golden retriever, like Rebel."

Phil and Doug both smiled and glanced down at their companions, murmuring her compliments to them.

Dean pointed to the two empty chairs next to Jess. "George, he's the organizer of the trip and leads the program we're all in, and his wife, Colleen, will be here soon. In addition to being wonderful people, they've been on several cruises, so they are a great help to those of us who are newbies." He smiled and added, "They also take pity on us being bachelors and make sure to sit with us at dinner."

They chatted about what they liked best about the cruise, with the food and the views coming in near the top of everyone's list. "Luckily, we all have the mini-suite cabins with balconies," said Dean, gesturing to Doug and Phil. "I'm not sure I could handle being in an inside cabin or one without a balcony. I know Rebel wouldn't like it."

Jess nodded. "I'm the same. I need to have access to fresh air and like the view it affords."

The waitstaff delivered bread and made sure everyone had water. Jess studied the menu and while everything sounded delicious, the potato soup and the roasted chicken and veggies caught her eye. As she was reading, George and Colleen arrived.

Jess pegged them to be in their seventies, both of them dressed to the nines for the evening, with him in a tux and Colleen wearing a shimmering gown in a bright blue that brought out her eyes. As they placed their orders and chatted, Colleen paid special attention to Jess.

Something about Colleen, her pale-blue eyes or maybe it was her mannerisms or just her calm wisdom, reminded Jess of her mom. As they chatted, the topic drifted to Jess' love of tea. Colleen asked if she had made plans to have Afternoon Tea on the ship.

"How did I not know about that option?" Jess smiled at the woman, who was excited to share.

"It's at three o'clock in the Crystal Dining Room. It's fun and something I always enjoy doing. Would you like to come with me? I'm planning to go when we get back on the ship from Ketchikan later in the week?"

"I'd love to go. Thanks for inviting me. I was hoping to go to The Empress for tea in Victoria, but we only have a few hours there and don't arrive until seven o'clock in the evening, so that won't work."

Colleen smiled and shook her head. "It's not near as posh as The Empress, but it is enjoyable. I, too, wish we had more time in Victoria. I would have loved to visit the gardens."

Jess raised her brows. "Oh, yes. That would have been fantastic. I enjoy flower gardening and haven't been to the Butchart Gardens for a long time. I guess I need to plan a visit to Victoria."

Colleen chuckled and glanced at Dean. "You'll be able to scoot over to Victoria easily once you start your new job on San Juan Island. I think it's only about an hour on the ferry."

Dean nodded as he took a sip of water. "I've never

been there but thought this stop would let me check it out and see if it's worth visiting again."

Jess turned toward him. "I haven't been for years, but it's a wonderful place to visit. Loads of things to do and see. That's exciting to be moving and starting a new job."

He gritted his teeth. "Exciting and a bit daunting at the same time. George helped me find what sounds like the perfect job, so I'm happy about that, but the whole moving thing has me a little anxious."

Their waiter arrived with the first course and made sure everyone had plenty of bread and refilled their glasses. Everyone turned their attention to their plates. Jess took her first spoonful of the potato soup, garnished with cheese and bacon. It was creamy and so satisfying.

While they ate, George talked a bit about the program he ran, Hope Foundation. Their mission was to assist veterans, especially those wounded, to realize their maximum potential as civilians. Counseling, help with finding suitable work, housing, peer support, connections with medical professionals, funding service dogs, and even making sure veterans had food, all fell under their umbrella.

As he spoke, Jess heard the passion in his voice and learned he was a Vietnam veteran. Dean and the other two men at the table were veterans of Afghanistan, having served in that conflict that started in 2001.

Their entrees arrived, and all conversation turned to critiquing the delicious selections before them. Jess eyed Dean's prime rib while she prepared to take her first bite of the roasted chicken and vegetables. The savory aroma of rosemary and garlic mingled with butter smelled divine.

As the meal progressed, the conversation shifted to the ship and points of interest. George and Colleen recommended the private pool and bar area on Deck 17 that was reserved for adults as a great spot to visit for a quieter experience. They were also big fans of the jazz lounge and planned to go there after dinner and listen to live music.

They had plans to play bingo in the casino and gave the wine bar a high recommendation. Colleen had planned several shore excursions and shared some of her favorite highlights at each of the port cities they would be visiting. Dean was right. They knew every inch of the ship and were full of ideas on what to do and see. After an ice cream sundae for dessert, Jess thanked Colleen for her recommendations.

"It's been my pleasure, Jess. I'm so pleased Dean invited you to join us. If we don't see you before, we'll see you here again for dinner."

Jess turned to Dean. "I'm stuffed and need to go for a bit of a walk." She put down her napkin and started to rise. "It's been wonderful meeting you all. Thank you for letting me crash your table."

While everyone said their goodbyes to Jess, Dean stood and pulled her chair back. "Are you up for some company? Rebel and I could also use a walk. I need to take him for a quick stop on Deck 10 first."

"Sure," she said, "and I wouldn't mind changing my shoes." She pointed at the sparkly sandals. "These aren't the best for walking."

"I'm all for changing into my jeans, too. I'm not much for fancy stuff. Rebel can make a pit stop in our cabin instead. How about you meet us at our cabin when you're ready, and we'll take a walk? I thought that planetarium show in the theatre Colleen mentioned might be a good choice for tonight."

"Sounds great. I'll be quick and see you down at your cabin. I'm just one deck above."

They took the elevator, and Dean and Rebel got off on Deck 11. "Cabin 410, sort of in the middle of the ship." He reminded her before the door closed.

She found another cute towel animal on her bed, this one a rabbit with floppy ears. She hung up her outfit and changed into a turtleneck and jeans, adding her puffy vest in case they spent time outside.

Within fifteen minutes, she was standing outside Dean's cabin, knocking on the door. He greeted her with a warm smile, wearing jeans and a gray V-neck shirt that accentuated the lightest strands of his hair. He opened the door wider and gestured for her to come inside. She looked around and said, "This is just like mine. My cabin is above yours, but next door." She pointed to the balcony. "I like that the balcony is a little larger since it angles out."

He nodded. "It comes in handy with Rebel. Gives us a bit more space for him."

She pointed at the towel animal on his bed, which was a bear with a cub. "I had a bunny tonight."

Dean chuckled. "The crew members are pretty creative, aren't they? If you gave me a couple of hours, I'm not sure I could make a towel animal."

He glanced at his watch. "It's later than I thought. I'm not sure we have time for a deck walk. Maybe we should go to the show and then take a walk after?"

"Sure, I'm fine with that."

He grabbed his jacket from the bed, motioned to

Rebel, and the dog was at his side in moments, ready to go.

They took the elevator down to the theatre and were shown to their seats. The show started less than ten minutes later, and they were surrounded by bright stars and the colorful lights of the Aurora Borealis that so many sought to see on trips to Alaska. The narrator, who was from the university in Anchorage explained how solar winds and solar storms react with Earth's magnetic field and create the gorgeous lights. She also said March was prime time to see them, so they would miss out on the real thing.

Jess was fascinated by the presentation and the dramatic field of stars surrounding them. In all her years of teaching, she didn't know that the sun's north and south poles swap places every eleven years. She loved the video presentation from the International Space Station that showed the variety of colors in the lights. The narrator explained how different gases in the atmosphere are excited by charged particles from the sun. The colors are determined by the type of gas the particles encounter. The most common green color is from oxygen, the beautiful purples, blues, and white are from nitrogen, and the rare red colors are from oxygen that is at higher altitudes.

The waves and spikes of colors and the soft music that played while they watched the constellations swirl around them were mesmerizing. The teacher in Jess loved learning new things, and her mind filled with lessons she could create using what she had discovered.

It was an automatic response, like breathing.

Her spirits sank a bit when she remembered she

wouldn't need to think of new and exciting lessons any longer.

After the show, they wandered to the café and picked up hot coffee drinks to keep them warm as they walked the decks. First, they wandered inside, window shopping along the Grand Atrium, taking the stairs as they ascended to each deck. Once they made it to Deck 17, they opted to sit on the small deck at the aft of the ship.

It offered a stunning view of the huge wake behind the ship. The Lido Deck below incorporated a pool and a bar in the same area, but the Sun Deck was quieter without those amenities. Despite the late hour, the sun was still low on the horizon, and the sky was only beginning to fade into dusk. They settled into chairs at a table to enjoy the panoramic sunset.

Jess took a sip from her cup and kept it in her hands. "Tell me about your new job. You never finished your story about moving to San Juan Island."

He sighed and sat back in his chair. "Yeah, I'm scheduled to be there in August. I've dabbled in photography and graphic arts for years. Drawing was something that helped when I was struggling years ago. I'm always doing things for the foundation, and George connected me with a guy who owns a real estate company there. Jack, that's the guy, made me an offer to handle the photography and drone footage for his listings, plus do the graphics for the website and social media. He's putting me up in a small place there, and I can use his equipment for side jobs. The pay isn't great, but it's more than enough to live on, especially with not having to pay rent."

"Wow, that sounds fantastic. It's such a beautiful place. I would imagine it's an artist and photographer's dream."

He smiled. "I haven't been since I was a kid and don't remember much, but I agree, the photo options are endless, and there is a thriving arts community throughout the islands."

"You mentioned you were uneasy about moving. What's got you worried?"

"Nothing specific. I think it's just change in general. It's a new place, and I won't know anybody. I'm old to be starting over, you know?" He chuckled, but Jess sensed the apprehension in his voice.

"I understand. I feel the same way about my new…" She put her cup down and made air quotes with her fingers, "freedom." She gazed out at the water. "Honestly, sometimes I think I should have just kept working and not retired. Like you, I think it's the change of routine that worries me. My life has been complicated this last year, especially."

"My life has been complicated for decades." He took a long swallow from his cup. "I lost my whole crew in Afghanistan. I survived, but years ago, I used to think it would have been better if I hadn't. It's been a tough road." He reached down and petted Rebel's back. "Having this guy and everyone at Hope Foundation has been life changing for me."

"I'm sorry for what you've been through." She shook her head. "That sounds weak, but I really mean it. I don't have any experience with what you've suffered. It breaks my heart to hear what you said, and I can't imagine the trauma you've been through."

He grinned. "That's a good thing. Nobody should ever imagine it. I appreciate your kindness. It's been a very long journey, but I'm in a good place now, and I think once I get in a groove with the new job and get settled, it will be good for me."

"At least you have a plan. I keep putting off thinking about what I'm going to do come August. I'm pretending this is just like any other summer vacation, but I'm scared. If Mom was…" Her voice caught, and the sting of tears burned in her throat.

His gentle eyes met hers. "You don't have to talk about it."

She nodded and swallowed more of her chocolate mocha before setting it on the table. She took a deep breath and spread her hands on her thighs. "I'm just going to say this really fast. I've been divorced for twelve years, and my mom came to live with me after Bruce left. She got sick a few years ago and died this February."

He reached for her hand and squeezed her fingers. "I'm so sorry, Jess."

She couldn't tell him the rest. Words escaped her. Instead of talking, she simply placed her hand in his and focused on the subtle pinks and purple hues that dusted the horizon as the sun dipped into the sea.

FOUR

Jess got back to her cabin late last night, having stayed up to play ball with Rebel and Dean after they walked the deck several times. Phil and Doug arrived with Ace and River and the three dogs ran around the court, leaping in the air to chase their balls and toys. Jess loved seeing the carefree play and their happy tails, but her heart ached, missing her sweet Ruby.

She couldn't wait to get to port later today and call Carly to check on her. Jess slipped into her exercise clothes and headed upstairs for a group class. She'd been thinking about joining a class when she got home and discovered the fitness center on board offered several. The view from the deck was inspiring as she tried to follow the instructor while she stretched and held the poses she demonstrated.

Most of the women in the class were fit and experienced. Jess was thankful she had chosen the back row, and her mistakes wouldn't be on display for everyone. She wasn't sure she was cut out for group classes. She needed to find one designed for out-of-shape, middle-aged women.

When the hour was up, she slipped to the stairway and headed back to her cabin. By the time she got there, she noticed the twinge in her thighs, coming from muscles she rarely used. She had plans to explore Juneau today, so they'd be getting even more of a workout.

A hot shower helped. She opted for a late breakfast so she wouldn't have to worry about finding time to eat lunch. She had booked a tour of the Alaska Capitol Building and then would need to catch the bus for her tour of the gardens and Mendenhall Glacier.

Jess steered clear of her favorite café with the croissants and went upstairs for the buffet. She filled her plate with eggs and bacon, passing up the pastries and choosing fruit, instead. People were coming and going, getting ready for the first port of call on the cruise and grabbing breakfast before the ship docked.

Jess finished her meal and after a stop to retrieve her jacket and the leather backpack, she went upstairs to the top deck to get a view of Juneau as the ship came into the pier. She wasn't the only one with that idea and had to hunt for a spot along the railing.

Dean had mentioned he wanted to get some shots from that viewpoint, but she didn't see him anywhere in the crowd of passengers. As the ship slowed and made its way to the dock, Jess took in the beauty of the heavy trees covering the land masses surrounding the narrow channel of water. It was stunning.

After taking several photos, Jess made her way downstairs. She wanted to be in the first group to disembark, since she had a full day of sightseeing ahead of her. Wisps of fog still hung in the air, and Jess was glad she had taken the advice to dress in layers. Despite the heavy layer of clouds, the weather forecast predicted partly sunny skies later in the day.

Jess never put too much stock in the forecasts and carried her retractable umbrella in her backpack. It took a bit of time to disembark, and Jess looked at the boardwalk to get her bearings. Juneau sat on the edge of the water, bordered by soaring mountains covered in trees, which had a dramatic effect. She took the route along the water, taking in the cute shops and restaurants that made up the tourist area. She had plenty of time to walk the few blocks and stopped to sit on a bench and put in a call to Carly.

She visited with her for a few minutes and asked about Ruby. Her heart felt lighter as she listened to Carly tell her all the fun they had been having playing in the yard and going for walks. She even sent her a picture of Ruby. "Give her big hugs from me," said Jess, her voice catching as she said goodbye. She couldn't believe how much she missed her furry friend.

She tucked her phone back in her pocket and in less than fifteen minutes, she made it to the Alaska State Capitol. Whenever she visited a new state, she tried to tour the capitol building. She enjoyed learning about the history and seeing the variety of architecture. When she stood on the street and studied the building, she was surprised. It lacked a dome and was rather plain, looking more like an office building than the center of government.

She took the steps to the entrance, graced by large marble pillars in front of the gold entry doors. Outside of these embellishments, the rest of the six-story building was without much ornamentation and rather small, by other standards. Without a dome or rotunda, there wasn't much of a focal point. The building did make use of beautiful wood and marble, but it didn't have the wow factor of so many buildings she had visited.

It didn't take Jess long to tour the entire facility and while doing so, she learned the building had served as the territorial offices when Alaska was a territory, prior to becoming a state in 1959. With the majority of states admitted to the union in the late 1700s and 1800s, Alaska was a rarity. The building was built in 1931 and half of the funding came from donations from the people of Alaska. That explained the lack of stunning architectural elements found in most capitol buildings.

The artwork in the building emphasized the culture and people of Alaska, with the use of Alaskan marble and references to the fishing, timber, and mining industries. Practicality and functionality were the words that came to mind as Jess toured the various rooms. She also learned there was a desire by some groups to construct a new capitol building in a grander style with a dome, but those efforts had failed.

Jess took a few photos and left, stopping to pick up a tea at a coffee shop on her way to the bus pickup at a nearby hotel. She had plenty of time to sip her drink and do a bit of people watching while she waited. The air was fresh and still a bit chilly, but the sun was trying to break through the clouds.

She hoped it held, as she would be outside the rest of the day. The ride to Mendenhall Glacier didn't take long. The small tour group had time to explore the glacier and Nugget Falls before catching the bus to spend time at the gardens. With several cruise ships docked, there were passengers on all the trails, and Jess recognized a few wearing lanyards and bracelets from the *Majestic Star*.

At the end of her hike, Jess was rewarded with spectacular falls thundering as they plunged almost four hundred feet into Lake Mendenhall. It was a definite photo opportunity and standing there made Jess feel rather small and insignificant, surrounded by such beauty and power.

She took in the blueish white ice of the glacier itself. The huge portion of ice she could see was nestled between two mountains, as if a river had been flowing and frozen in time. Jess had no desire to trek across it or canoe out to see it up close and personal. She took a few photos of it and wandered back to get on the bus, anxious to visit the gardens.

In addition to garden tours, the owners operated a nursery and landscaping business, which was how they got their start in the area. Jess boarded a tram and enjoyed the winding pathways through the forest and botanical garden. The bright azaleas and rhododendrons were stunning against the green foliage that dominated the forest areas. The garden was known for its upside-down trees that were old logs serving as flower pots, spilling with colorful blooms at the top.

The tram took the group up Thunder Mountain, which offered a panoramic view down to the harbor below. As they made the trip up the incline, the sun disappeared, replaced by clouds. Jess could make out the cruise ship and when she turned the other direction, she could see the airport. From her vantage point, it was even easier to see how the town sat in a small pocket surrounded by dramatic peaks and dark waters.

She could only imagine it in winter when it snowed. It would be beautiful nestled in the snowy mountains. Living on Mercer Island, they only received a few inches of snow each year. Juneau received more than ten times their average and double the amount of rain. As the tour guide talked about the weather, it began to sprinkle.

It was a gentle shower, and Jess flipped up the hood on her jacket while she captured photos of the colorful plants that caught her eye. The tram stopped at the gift shop and visitor center, and Jess perused the offerings but didn't see anything she couldn't live without. Remembering all the totes of classroom stuff she had collected over three decades, she vowed not to come home with too many souvenirs.

The visitor center atrium was decorated with several hanging baskets of vibrant flowers and lush climbing plants along the trellis. It was still raining and had morphed into a heavier downpour by the time they loaded into the bus to head back to town. The ride took less than thirty minutes and dropped her on the street that led to the cruise terminal. The ship wasn't leaving until well after dinner. She wasn't sure whether to find something to eat in Juneau or head back to the ship and eat there.

The streets were crowded with tourists rushing to find restaurants and cafés to escape the rain. The mass of people made her decision easy. She unearthed her umbrella and headed back to the ship. Her cell phone chimed, and she dug it out of her pocket while she continued to walk.

She grinned as she glanced at the message from Dean. They had exchanged phone numbers last night, knowing they probably wouldn't cross paths, since he and his group were set up on a wildlife and hiking excursion. He was letting her know he would be back on the ship soon and wondered if she wanted to meet up for dinner.

By the time she reached the ship, it was raining even harder. Happy she had worn her rain gear and boots, she stepped on board, anxious to find a place to get warm and find something hot to drink. She visited her favorite café on Deck 5 and ordered a chai tea latte, resisting the decadent pastries flirting with her from the case.

While she waited for her latte, she texted Dean back and let him know she was on the ship and would meet him for dinner but suggested a later seating. The atrium was almost empty of cruisers, which was a nice change. Despite the hot latte, Jess was still chilled. Dean texted back that he was fine with a later time for dinner.

She took the elevator to the dining room and inquired about changing her seating to a later time. With the majority of the passengers off the ship, the hostess said it was no problem. Jess headed back to her cabin, donned her swimsuit and a robe, and headed back up to Deck 17 for a soak in the hot tub in the adult area. The rain had let up and was a gentle sprinkle again.

With the decks almost empty, this was the perfect time to take advantage of a bit of privacy. A few people were at the bar, but she had the hot tub to herself. She slid into the warm water and sighed. As the water bubbled around her, and the jets helped to loosen the muscles in her back, she closed her eyes.

Contacting Carly, and knowing Ruby was doing okay,

lifted a weight she had been carrying. Getting off the ship and taking in the scenery had been a nice break, but the slosh of the warm water against her skin was pure heaven. She didn't even notice the rain as she rested her head against the side and let her body relax.

As much as she didn't want to ever leave, after thirty minutes, she climbed out. The cool air made her shiver as steam rolled off her skin. She reached for her robe and snuggled into it and stuffed her feet into her outdoor slippers. She felt like a new woman.

She took the elevator back to her cabin and jumped into the shower. An hour later, she was dressed, and her hair was dried and curled. Not having eaten much of anything since breakfast, she was starving when she arrived at the dining room. Tonight, the hostess led her to a table for two, where she found Dean and Rebel waiting.

Again, Dean stood and moved her chair for her. "How was your day?" he asked.

"It was a fun time. I enjoyed getting to see the gardens and walk around downtown, but the best part of my day was checking on Ruby." She smiled as she thanked the waiter for the water he poured.

"I'm glad to hear she's doing well." He glanced down at Rebel. "We had a good day, but it was a long trek, and then the rain wasn't the best." He scanned the menu options while they chatted. "I did get some awesome photos, though."

They both opted for soup and ordered their entrees, and Jess asked for a pot of hot tea. Rebel snoozed while they ate and enjoyed the almost empty dining room, with most passengers opting to visit restaurants in town.

As they lingered over desserts, Dean set his cup of

coffee on the saucer. "You mentioned you were divorced. Do you have children?"

Jess finished her sip of tea and smiled. "I have one son Jake. He's grown and lives near his dad in Maine. That's where my ex-husband's family is and where he moved to when we divorced. Jake is twenty-seven now." She rubbed her fingers on the edge of her napkin. Despite so many years, the shame and pain of it all still hurt. "What about you?"

Dean shook his head. "No, sadly, no children. No wife. I came close years ago with a fiancée, but that ended in a wreck. My fault. After I returned from Afghanistan, I wasn't myself. Things went downhill quickly, and Laurie couldn't take it. I don't blame her."

Jess met his eyes, filled with sadness. "I'm sorry, Dean. I'm sure on top of everything else you were dealing with, that was beyond difficult for you."

He nodded and reached for Rebel at his feet. "I write to her from time to time. She was kind enough to continue to be my friend, but she married, had kids, has a life of her own now."

"I think I've only gone on two dates since Bruce and I divorced. They were forced outings that my friends pushed me into. They were both disasters, and I've elected to fill my days with work and gardening."

"Did Jake come to stay with you for the summers?"

She looked down at the tablecloth. "No, sadly, he sided with his dad. He was almost fifteen when we divorced, and I wasn't about to force him to spend time with me. He came for a couple of weeks that first summer, but it was clear he didn't want to be there. I always extended an invitation to him for holidays and summer vacations, but he's rarely taken me up on the offer. Sometimes I feel like I've lost him forever."

The burning sensation in her throat made her reach for her cup again. She swallowed a few sips and then gazed out the window. "If I had known, I would have to sacrifice Jake in the divorce, I probably would have just stayed married. It would have been hard, but I'll always wonder if it would have made a difference."

Dean took another sip of coffee and a bit of his cake. "Regrets are hard to live with. I've learned to limit the time I spend on them and the same goes for living in the past. It's hard when it feels like that's where my life stopped, but I'm trying to live in the present and find a new path forward."

She nodded. "I thought I was doing okay, until this year. Losing Mom has been the worst. I'm not sure I'll ever get over it. We were very close, and now my house just feels empty. Not to mention the huge hole in my heart. It's hard to be there with all her memories but not her."

Dean reached across the table for her hand. "I know what you mean. I lost my mom several years ago. I blame myself for that, too. I think watching me implode took its toll on her. After that, my dad and I drifted apart. He moved to Florida to be closer to my sister and her kids, plus he has a sister of his own nearby."

He pulled his hand back and pushed his half-eaten cake to the side. "Dad's happy there, which makes me happy. He likes the weather, plays golf, and lives in a retirement community. The last thing I want to do is feel like a burden to him. Like he was staying around just for me."

Jess pressed her lips together. "I'm sure he doesn't think of you as a burden. It's hard to watch your kids suffer and be powerless to help."

He shrugged. "After I came home, albeit broken, I think he saw me as weak. He never said it in so many words, but that's the feeling I got. He was proud of me being in the military. He had served, and I think seeing what happened to me, embarrassed him or something. I'm not sure. His generation is tough and stoic and thinks of vulnerability as a weakness."

He welcomed Rebel's head onto his thigh, petting the top of it. "Dad, I'm sure, thought I would get better, and things would go back to normal. When they didn't and Mom got sick, things spiraled downward quickly. My decision to pursue graphic arts and photography didn't sit well either. I fear I'm a disappointment and with us so far apart, he doesn't have to see it on a daily basis."

Jess' heart ached for Dean as his words resonated with her. She wondered if part of Jake felt the same way about her. They were far apart and didn't see one another but once a year if they were lucky. Somehow, he decided to blame her for the divorce. Nothing could be further from the truth, and no matter what she said, he wouldn't budge from his belief. Year after year, she had clung to the hope that Jake would find his way back to her. Back home. But it hadn't happened yet.

She had no wise advice for Dean. No soothing words that would make things better. She had enjoyed a close relationship and friendship with her mom and could only imagine the heartbreak he endured missing his dad.

She took a long swallow from her cup. "I think it's hard to know what other people want from us. All we can do is our best, and I think the idea of using your skills to pursue something new and exciting in your life is a great step forward for your future. Maybe once you're settled in and feeling good about your new routine, you can invite your dad to visit."

He nodded, and she noticed the glint of tears in his eyes.

"I think we need a distraction. Are you up for line dancing?" she asked. "I found out they're doing a class in the atrium tonight. I thought it might be a fun way to exercise."

He rolled his eyes. "Honestly, my first reaction is it sounds close to the ninth circle of hell. But you look excited about it, and I like spending time with you, so I'll go."

She laughed and accepted his hand when he moved to help her from her chair. Jess continued to hold his hand as they left the dining room. It had been a long time since she had felt that warmth in her palm. She wasn't sure she even missed it.

Until now.

FIVE

It took Dean a few songs to get into the line dancing routine, but it seemed to grow on him. By the end of the night, he was even smiling.

Not only did Jess and Dean line dance until late into the evening, but then they took Rebel to the upper deck so he could exercise and play ball with River and Ace. She noticed Dean was limping slightly but didn't draw attention to it. After a stop at the café for hot tea, and a leisurely stroll, it was after one o'clock in the morning when Jess returned to her cabin. By the time she fell into bed, she was exhausted.

That, Jess reasoned, was why she'd overslept and when she opened her eyes, did a double take. She squinted and finally slipped on her reading glasses. It was almost nine o'clock. She couldn't remember the last time she had slept so late.

The ship was due in Skagway early in the morning and luckily, Jess had no planned excursions. The only thing on her agenda for the day was another check-in on Ruby and a bit of exploring of Skagway on her own.

Dean was taking a photography outing and was sure to have left the ship by now. Jess opted to order room service, which arrived shortly after she finished getting ready for the day. She enjoyed the meal on her balcony, which provided a beautiful but chilly morning view of the Inside Passage. She took a few photos from her balcony and sent one to Jake.

Once done with her omelet, she put in a video call to Carly so she could get a look at her sweet girl. Ruby's ears perked when she heard Jess' voice. Carly assured Jess they were doing fine, and Ruby was getting lots of attention. Anyone watching might find it ridiculous that she was so happy to talk to her dog on the video call, but Jess' heart lightened when she saw her best friend. It was difficult to have a prolonged conversation with Ruby, but Jess loved seeing her smile and the tilt of her ears when Ruby heard her voice. The lump in Jess' throat grew as she said goodbye. Ruby looked happy, but Jess couldn't help but miss her.

To distract herself from the emptiness, she focused on the brochure with information about Skagway and things to do in the area. Shopping and tours dominated the offerings.

On her way out, Jess stopped at the café for a latte and then headed to the pier, her worn leather backpack with her. The charming small town nestled in the pocket of the Sawtooth Mountains resembled something from an old-time Western movie set. The storefronts consisted of Gold Rush-era buildings, with signs advertising eateries, coffee shops, souvenirs, arts, and tours.

It was a cloudy day, and Jess had her trusty umbrella, despite no rain in the forecast. Jess browsed a few shops and noticed a tour for a garden drumming up customers and made a spontaneous choice to join the group. They only had a few people in the van and offered Jess a great deal on the price. The van took them on a quick two-mile drive up the Klondike Highway.

Their tour guide welcomed them to the lush gardens and gave them maps of the property, highlighting the gift shop and restaurant. The smiling woman led them on the pathway, telling the group about the history of the gardens and Skagway, known as the Garden City of Alaska.

The small group wandered the paths that took them to different areas throughout the garden, where a variety of plants and flowers were showcased. Jess took in the beautiful colors of the flowering plants and the imposing mountains that made for a dramatic backdrop. She snapped photo after photo and had a hard time tearing herself away from the stunning peonies in the conservatory. They were one of her favorite flowers, and the gorgeous pinks and deep reds on display were some of the best she had seen.

With some time to explore on their own, Jess took a break in their lovely tea room and enjoyed a pot of Earl Grey while she relaxed and soaked in the ambience of the view. After nibbling on the cookie that came with her tea, Jess set out for the glass-blowing studio and demonstration.

She had visited the Chihuly Garden and Glass several times. It had been one of her mom's favorite outings. She stepped into the space, warmed by the glowing furnaces where the glass blowers did their work. While this garden was small by comparison to Chihuly, Jess was mesmerized as she watched the artists work with the molten glass. Jess found the entire process hypnotic. As the artists manipulated the fluid glass, sometimes so limp it looked like it would fall, into shape and then drizzled colored glass on top of it, she couldn't force her eyes away.

It was fascinating to see the entire process from start to finish and watch as they rolled the glass across metal tables and blew into the long tubes that created bubbles of glass that grew and changed shape in front of her eyes. The deft and confident moves the artists made were a testament to their skill and experience.

As they worked, the tour guide narrated and explained some of the processes and how minerals were often added to glass to give it color, and Jess was surprised to learn that the cranberry glass she was fond of was actually made by adding gold to clear glass.

The staff treated everyone to refreshments and invited them to visit with the artists and check out some of their recent work. After the wonderful demonstration, Jess couldn't resist a quick stop in the gift shop where she bought a gorgeous glass heart in the beautiful pink glass she loved. The clerk wrapped it with bubble wrap and tissue and made sure it was tucked into a box.

After a few more photos, Jess boarded the van, and it whisked them back to town and dropped them on the main street. Jess walked by an ice cream shop and was powerless to withstand the urge to step inside. She left with a smile, toting her homemade waffle cone stuffed with strawberry ice cream.

She had polished it off by the time she got back to the ship. As was the case yesterday, the atrium area was almost empty of passengers. A creature of habit, Jess made a stop at the café and had a bowl of soup and some fruit before she returned to her cabin. She and Dean had a late dinner seating, and the ice cream wasn't quite enough to satisfy her until then.

After another soak in the hot tub on the upper deck, she read her book and dozed, waking up in time to get ready for dinner. It was odd not to have somewhere to be or something she had to do. Despite having summers off, she had filled them with activities related to her classroom, always making plans for interesting lessons for her students. This was a taste of her new normal, and Jess wasn't sure if she liked it or not.

She would have to find something to do when she got home, or she would go stir crazy sitting around the house. She needed to give it a good cleaning out and go through her mom's things, but she wasn't sure she was ready for that. She had a stack of books to read and loved spending time with her flower garden, but she had to find something to fill the hours in the day.

She made a mental note to look into volunteer opportunities. She flipped to her messages on her phone, and her shoulders sagged. Jake hadn't replied to her photo and earlier message. She had to make more of an effort to connect with him but wasn't sure how to do it. His repeated rebuffs didn't boost her confidence. He had his own life, but she hoped now that she had a free schedule, she could find a way to visit more often.

The thought of their almost non-existent relationship brought the sting of tears to her eyes. She vowed to do better and put more effort in, especially now that her mom was gone. She had been her focus these past years, and that made it difficult to travel. Jake did come last year and visited with his grandma, who had loved him dearly. He didn't stay long enough to suit Jess, but his presence had brought a smile to her mother's face and for that, she was grateful.

Being divorced so long, Jess had gotten used to spending much of her time alone, but she felt the tickle of panic in the back of her mind when she tried to picture her days of retirement. That niggle of fear of the empty days ahead was unexpected. She had only considered the good parts of being obligation free when she made her decision to retire.

She checked her phone once more, then grabbed her jacket and set out for the dining room. Dean was already seated when the hostess led her to their table. He was staring out the window and didn't notice her arrival, but Rebel did.

Dean smiled and stood to pull out her chair. "You looked deep in thought," she said, placing the napkin across her lap. "Did you have a good day?"

"It was a good day. A long one, but I was able to get tons of great shots."

After placing their orders and getting their first course of soup, Jess told him about her day at the gardens and the glass-blowing studio. "Sounds like you had fun. I'm sort of glad tomorrow is a day on the ship. I'm tired of the schedule and the long days." He glanced down at Rebel. "I think Rebel could use a day of relaxing, too."

She nodded. "I saw they are having some park rangers come aboard tomorrow, and they will be giving talks and answering questions about Glacier Bay National Park. There's also a group bringing sled dog puppies aboard. I'm excited about that."

"I hope to be able to get some decent shots from the upper deck tomorrow, but I think I'll be laying low for the most part. These early mornings are getting old." He ruffled Rebel's ears. "Especially when we stay up late to make sure he gets to play on the court each night."

The waiter delivered their meals, and Dean told her more about his day of hiking and traveling to the top of the summit. The circles under his eyes matched the tiredness in his voice.

"At least you have a good reason to be tired. For not doing much, I'm feeling rather bushed today and even took a nap this afternoon." She took a sip of water. "I think it's mental exhaustion for me. I've been doing lots of thinking and am nervous about the future. I've never had this much free time."

They ordered hot tea to accompany their dessert. Dean sat back in his chair and sighed. "I think I'm struggling with unease about the future, too. I'm excited about being able to do something I enjoy, but at the same time, terrified I'll lose my stable routine here, and all the work I've put in could be for nothing."

Jess smiled at him. "I have a feeling George wouldn't recommend you or help you get set up with this new job if he didn't think you were ready. It sounds like he has years of experience and only has your best interest at heart."

Dean bobbed his head as he ran his finger along the rim of his cup. "You're right. He's told me that same thing. He's confident I'm ready, and I know they need the space in the group home I've been living in. Honestly, it will be great to have my own space and more autonomy." He sighed. "I just don't know that I can handle a failure."

"Just remember almost everything is fixable, so a setback isn't a failure." She poured more tea into her cup.

He chuckled. "You're right, of course. Part of what George teaches us is centered around that idea. The type of work I did, there was zero room for failure. A setback usually meant something had gone horribly wrong. It's hard to dial down that intensity. That's been a big part of what I've been working on and why I gravitated to photography and graphic arts. It's the best example of being able to rework and fix almost anything, especially with all the digital tools we use now."

"I'm a big proponent of finding something you enjoy doing and if you can make a living at it, that's a true gift." She folded the edges of her napkin back and forth. "Not having a purpose now because I truly did love teaching and my students, worries me."

"Oh, I get that. Coming home, dealing with the loss of so many brothers and friends, nothing matched that mission or purpose we had. Realizing life would never be that exciting or that harrowing again is both a plus and a minus, in a weird way."

"I'm definitely going to look for some volunteer opportunities when I get home. I've got some chores to get through, but once that's done, I have to find a purpose beyond cleaning and reading."

His brows rose. "You ought to talk to George and Colleen. They're always looking for volunteers." He shrugged. "Not sure it would be up your alley, but it's an idea."

She nodded. "That's a good idea. I should have thought of it before now. I was thinking about the animal shelter, but then I thought I'd go crazy and want to rescue all of them. The library and of course, the schools, are always looking for volunteers, but something different is also appealing."

She noticed him rubbing his leg, his teeth gritted.

"Are you okay? I thought we might have overdone it line dancing."

He grinned. "Just showing my age. Too much hiking, plus the dancing probably didn't help."

They finished off the tea, and Dean stood and offered Jess his hand. "You mentioned the appeal of something new. If you get too bored, you can always make the trip over to San Juan Island and visit me. I'd enjoy seeing a familiar face." He led the way up the stairs to the upper decks.

She noticed the gleam in his eye. "Be careful, I might just take you up on that idea. This trip reminds me of the beauty of that area, and I'll have plenty of time on my hands for trips."

"My door is always open to you, Jess."

"As long as I can bring my sweet Ruby. I'm having serious withdrawals."

"Of course, Ruby would be welcome. In fact, maybe when we get home, we can arrange to meet up and let Ruby meet Rebel. I'll be around until the middle of August when I move."

"It's a date," said Jess. The words flew out of her mouth before she could think. Her cheeks burned, and she couldn't deny the flutter of excitement at the prospect of spending more time with Dean.

SIX

They made their way to the upper deck where despite the evening still filled with sunlight, a movie was playing on the large screen. Dean and Rebel led the way to a quiet spot outside of the audience area. Almost as soon as they sat, a staff member appeared with warm blankets and the offer of a hot beverage, popcorn, and cookies.

They both opted for hot chocolate and settled under the cozy blankets. Rebel relaxed and lounged on the deck next to Dean's chair. With a long sigh, Dean rested his head against the back of the chair. "It's a beautiful evening up here." He checked his watch. "We'll be setting sail soon."

"Do you need to get your camera?"

He grinned and shook his head. "I think I've photographed every angle of this place today."

The waiter returned with their hot chocolates, plus a small tray with extra marshmallows, peppermint sticks, and a few cookies. Jess took a sip. "Mmm, not bad. I can't remember ever sipping hot chocolate in the summer, but it's perfect for our chilly evening."

Dean smiled. "There's never a wrong time for hot chocolate, right? It always reminds me of being a kid; my mom would make it on the stovetop for us as an after-school treat."

"You mentioned you had a sister in Florida. Is she older?"

He nodded. "Yes, Debbie is three years older. It's the age-old phenomenon. She's the apple of my dad's eye, and I was that same to my mom. She has three grown kids with grandkids, and they all live within a few hours of her."

"I'm sure your dad enjoys that. Did you consider moving there instead of staying in this area?"

He looked down at his cup. "Not really. Dad asked me to, offered to help me, but I don't want to do that. It's an option that's there for me if I need it."

"I love the Pacific Northwest and don't ever see myself leaving. I've wrestled with that, more so lately, now that I have the freedom to leave. I wish I was closer to my son." She glanced over the deck and to the mountains. "I also think even if I undertook moving, it wouldn't change much between the two of us. I'm trying to figure out how to foster a better relationship between us, hoping I can visit Jake soon."

He drummed his fingers on the edge of the table. "I'm not sure why, but families sure can be tricky. I sometimes tell myself things would be better if my mom were still here. She was the center of our family. I think Dad left because he couldn't bear it here without her and being near Debbie and her family is the next best thing for him. I wasn't much of a son for many years."

Jess saw the regret in Dean's eyes and swallowed the lump in her throat that had formed while he talked. "You need to be gentle with yourself. What you endured was horrific. I'm sure you did the best you could, and your energy had to go to focus on your own survival. I bet your dad understands that, even if he was disappointed at the time."

Dean nodded but didn't say anything.

She met his eyes. "I know how easy it is to blame yourself and look back on regrets. I've done that for years, especially when it comes to my son. I've had hundreds of students over the course of my career and with the exception of a handful, I have loved teaching them. I get notes from them when they're older telling me how much they enjoyed my class and still get invited to their graduations and weddings. In addition to making me feel old, it makes me sad to think somehow, I succeeded with them but failed my own son. It can be overwhelming."

His shoulders slumped a bit. "Guilt is a horrible monster. I'm in a continual battle with the beast."

Jess' throat tightened, and she reached for her cup. "I do okay during the day, but when I go to bed, thoughts rush through my mind. I can't shut them off. Not only do I feel guilty about Jake, but I have a sister out there somewhere. At least I think I do. For all I know, she could be dead. I haven't seen her or talked to her in decades."

Dean's eyes grew wider. "I'm so sorry, Jess. That would be awful."

Jess took in a deep breath. "Erin is ten years younger, sort of a surprise for my parents. She was a sweet little girl but very spoiled by Mom and Dad. Things took a downward spiral in high school, and Erin got into lots of trouble. I was out of the house by then and had my own life with a baby on the way, so I wasn't that involved. I just saw the toll it took on my parents."

She glanced at the movie screen and then continued, "Erin talked Mom and Dad into a gap year, putting off college. She and her friends had a plan to travel, and that was the beginning of the end. She didn't keep in contact much and when she did, it was by postcard. She didn't bother to call my parents on birthdays or holidays. She always had an excuse. She was supposed to be home for Christmas but didn't come and didn't call."

Her voice cracked, and she took a long sip of hot chocolate. "Mom and Dad were devastated. Erin drifted further away, and they turned her in as a missing person when they hadn't heard from her in the months that followed Christmas. It was gut wrenching to watch them suffer. I think it led to my dad's ultimate demise."

"Did the police have any luck finding her?"

She shook her head. "No, and they told my parents she was an adult and had every right to disappear if she wanted to do so. I think they took the report and added her to the system, but the last time she had talked to my parents, she had been in New York. Not much the police here could do about that, and it wasn't like they suspected she had been abducted. My parents had no idea what she was doing or where she was, so very few leads for them to follow."

"So, did she ever come home?"

"For my dad's funeral. That's the last time she was here. She happened to call, and Mom pleaded with her to come home. He was terminal, and his time was short. Of course, Erin didn't make it in time to see him, but at least she was home for the funeral."

The sun set as the ship moved away from the pier. "It was hard on my mom. Erin had lots of piercings and tattoos, along with wild-colored hair. She didn't resemble the sweet girl in the photo Mom kept framed on her dresser. She stayed long enough to talk Mom out of some money and then disappeared again."

"Wow," said Dean, with his brows arched high. "Your poor mom."

"She struggled. I didn't understand quite how much until Jake left and chose to live with his dad. Erin had no interest in me, Mom, not even her nephew, whom she had never met until then. I wrote her off and have resented her for years. She broke Mom's heart, and I'm convinced she was the cause of Dad's illness."

Dean finished off his hot chocolate and pushed the cup toward the middle of their small table. "I never wanted to disappoint my parents. I did some dumb stuff growing up but nothing extreme. I missed my family the entire time I was in the military. You sort of develop a substitute family with your team, especially in the unit I was in. We became closer than brothers. It was nice to have that feeling of belonging so far away, but I lived for those times when I could get leave and come home to visit my family. Things changed after the attack. It broke something inside me. Something I'm not sure I can ever glue back together."

It was dark enough she couldn't see his face clearly, but in the soft lighting from the deck, she noticed the sheen of tears in his eyes. She looked up at the star-filled sky and swallowed hard, but the lump was still there. "I'm not sure it's possible to ever get over a trauma, much less the multiple traumas you witnessed and the horrible grief of losing so many of your team members."

He looked down at Rebel. "Survivor's guilt is hard to explain. Everyone thinks you're lucky, but all I felt was shame. I made the mistake so many of us do and turned to booze to dull the pain. To escape."

He rested his hand on the top of Rebel's head. "Those images can't be unseen. They're part of me. Forever. Finally, with George's guidance, I've been able to deal with things in a better way. The last ten years have been a struggle, but now, I'm at least able to say I'm thankful to be alive. I wish I could have figured things out before losing my mom."

Jess reached for his hand. "I think she knows. I feel my mom with me all the time." She squeezed his hand tighter and lowered her voice. "Sometimes, I even find myself talking to her."

He grinned and swiped at a tear on his cheek. "Your secret's safe with me."

The next morning was another lazy one for Jess. She had stayed up late enough to accompany Dean and Rebel to the court where they threw the ball for the dog to let him exercise and have a bit of fun. After their somber conversation about regrets and guilt, it didn't feel right to leave Dean on his own.

It had been years since she had shared a meaningful conversation with a man. She had relied on her mom for support ever since she and Bruce had divorced and losing her had left Jess feeling adrift. She had her work friends, but she never got too close to any of them. Since her divorce, she had withdrawn and had no close friends with whom she felt comfortable to bare her soul. Her mom had been that special friend for her and without her, it was hard to cope.

Dean was different. Maybe because he didn't know her. Maybe because they shared a similar pain. Maybe because it was easier to talk to him, and he didn't judge or tell her what she should do like so many of her teacher friends did. She found talking to him effortless and a soothing balm to her broken heart.

She pulled back the heavy curtains to let the daylight fill her cabin, squinting at the brightness. Today, the ship would be bustling, as there were no excursions while they sailed by Glacier Bay National Park. The cruise line had organized guest lecturers and activities for the passengers, and Jess was looking forward to the sled dog puppies and listening to the park ranger discussions.

Dean would be on a top deck taking photos most of the day or relaxing on his cabin balcony, and they made plans to meet up for dinner, unless they bumped into each other earlier.

It was mid-morning by the time Jess was ready for the day. She knew the ship would be packed and didn't relish the idea of crowded hallways or restaurants. She opted to order breakfast and sit on the balcony to take in the views of the park. The ship was broadcasting some of the ranger talks on the television system, so she tuned to the channel while she waited for room service.

It was a cloudy day, but the aquamarine water that

reminded Jess of the pale pieces of sea glass she had collected, was beautiful. Breakfast arrived, and she bundled into her jacket and took it outside so she could eat while she watched for wildlife and glaciers.

As the ship went through the narrow passage, the rangers pointed out specific formations and drew attention to the seals sitting atop chunks of ice in the water. Jess captured a few photos, catching herself when she thought of showing them to her mom. She loved animals and would have enjoyed them.

Her mom dominated her thoughts today. She tried to concentrate on the awe-inspiring glaciers, made of ice with a vivid blue tint to it. Even the dramatic caving they witnessed when a huge piece of ice fell into the water and created a wave she felt hit the ship, didn't totally distract her.

She wasn't sure how she would handle her much-too-empty house. Thank goodness she had Ruby.

As it began to rain, Jess moved inside her cabin. She was chilled to the bone and needed something hot to drink.

After taking the stairs for exercise, she found herself on Deck 5 at the little café she liked. She took her large chai tea and set out to roam the ship. There were educational talks taking place in the theatre, but she didn't feel like sitting and couldn't seem to concentrate.

She ducked into the talk and display of sled dog puppies. They were so cute and cuddly, but the place was packed with people and every kid on the ship. She already missed Ruby and suspected a roomful of puppies might just make it worse.

She needed something to do. Something to occupy her

mind. A colorful sign for a paint and sip event in one of the lounges caught her eye. She made her way to it and found out it started in fifteen minutes.

She took a seat at the end of a row, in front of an easel, prepped and ready for painting. She studied the sample of the canvas they would all be painting. The gorgeous dark skies filled with the colors of the Northern Lights and the tall trees below made for an eye-catching painting. She wasn't confident in her abilities, but it would give her something to concentrate on and keep her occupied.

A server came along the rows of seats and offered beverages. Despite the early afternoon hour, several cruisers chose wine or cocktails. Jess stuck with hot tea and settled in to do a bit of people watching while she waited for the instructor to begin.

Most of the people in the class were in small groups or twosomes. Jess' heart beat faster as she realized she was the only one on her own. She never thought of herself as being alone, since she was always with Ruby, but the harsh reality was right in front of her.

She watched as people wandered in, but nobody took the empty chair next to hers.

Staff members moved through the room and delivered plastic palettes of acrylic paints, the wells already filled with the colors they would be using—blue, white, black, green, and purple. They also provided three different brushes and a cup of water for washing them.

Her eyes settled on a group of older women two rows in front of her, who were laughing and enjoying themselves, imbibing in a bit of wine, while they waited. She hoped she would be like them when she was their age. Who was she kidding? She wasn't even close to their level, and she was at least twenty years younger. She needed to up her game.

The instructor, who introduced herself as Jasmine, started speaking, and Jess turned her attention to the front of the lounge. Jasmine's canvas was shown on several screens around the room, so it was easy to see what she was doing from any seat.

As she began to work with the paint, Jess relaxed. It was easier than she thought, and the instructor explained each step before she demonstrated the technique on her canvas. Jasmine had a calm way about her and stressed for each of them to add as much or little color as they wanted to make the painting their own. She showed them how to blend the dark night sky with the lighter horizon.

The more Jess painted, especially using the easy technique Jasmine showed them to make realistic tree branches, the more her spirits lifted. The group of ladies she had her eye on was having lots of fun. They seemed to be playing some sort of drinking game, sipping more than painting, giggling the entire time.

Jess smiled. They were too cute.

By the time she was at the last step and adding in tiny dots of white to represent the stars, Jess was immersed in the project and forgot her worries about being on her own. Despite her fears, nobody was pointing and making fun of her or even seemed to notice she was alone.

How many times had she counseled one of her students about worrying over something that didn't really matter? Or told them not to concern themselves too much with what other people thought about them? Here she was, fifty-something, self-conscious and worrying about being judged by people she would never see again.

This lost feeling she had was new. It had come with the passing of her mother. If she were honest, probably in the months before when she saw the harsh writing on the wall. Jess had always been good at putting one foot in front of the other, taking things as they came, pushing aside her worries and embracing her work and her students.

As her mother grew older and their roles reversed, Jess realized her world would change. When the diagnosis came, and there wasn't much hope, Jess began to unravel. After Bruce left, and Jake chose to live with him, she built a new life with her mom. Her mom filled the void losing them had left in her heart.

The thought of being without her shook Jess to her core. Her mom was accepting and had made her peace with the situation, but Jess wasn't ready. She didn't expect she would ever be ready. People often say losing someone to a long illness is easier than other ways, giving them time to prepare.

Jess wasn't convinced.

She'd been busy these last few weeks, first trying to finagle a way out of the cruise and then getting everything ready for the trip. She wasn't sure how she would deal with life when she got home. Ruby, of course, would be of great comfort, but just thinking about being in her house, without her mom, was suffocating.

She had to find something new to do. She looked at her finished canvas and while it was passable, she was sure she wouldn't be taking the Seattle art scene by storm.

SEVEN

After returning to her cabin for a nap, Jess changed her clothes, fluffed her hair, and touched up her face. The ship was well underway to the next port and due to arrive early in the morning in Ketchikan. With all the passengers onboard, the dining rooms would be busy.

She wore jeans and comfy shoes and set out on the stairs to the Pearl Dining Room. Dean and his faithful dog were already seated at their table, along with Phil and River and Doug with Ace. George and Colleen were missing, but Colleen's wrap was on the back of her chair.

The men stood as soon as Jess reached the table, and Dean pulled her chair out for her. "Such gentlemen," she said with a smile. She asked about their day, which all three of them confessed to spending relaxing in their cabins or on their balconies when they weren't taking their dogs for a jaunt around the ship.

Dean reached for his glass of water. "I did get some great shots of the glaciers and some wildlife today. It was nice that they had the commentary on the television, so I captured most of my photos from the balcony."

"It was a bit of a lazy day for me, too," Jess said, after asking for a pot of hot tea. "I did go to a paint and sip event, and it was fun."

Colleen and George appeared right before the server came to take their orders. Colleen turned to Jess. "Now, I trust you're set to join me for tea tomorrow at three o'clock. I'm looking forward to it."

Jess nodded. "Yes, I've got a reminder set. That should be a fun afternoon."

Colleen quizzed her about her excursions and if she was enjoying the cruise. Jess rubbed the edge of the napkin between her fingers. "Honestly, it's not as bad as I thought it would be. I just miss my dog Ruby. While we were in port, I put in a call so I could talk to my dog sitter and get to see my sweet girl on the video. I can't wait to get home and have her next to me." She sighed. "It's helped to meet Rebel and his friends, though."

"They are marvelous dogs, aren't they? Truly transformational in what they do for our veterans."

The server returned with their starters and as they enjoyed soup, Colleen continued chatting, telling Jess she went to an exercise class and then spent most of the day in the spa being pampered.

She leaned over and whispered to her husband and then smiled at Jess. "I have a seat on the float plane excursion tomorrow and wondered if you would be interested in taking it? I ran into two ladies, and we've made some plans for tomorrow. I totally forgot about the trip. You'd be with these four gentlemen and the three dogs."

"Oh, wow. Uh, I don't know."

Dean caught her eye. "I think it's only about an hour, maybe a little more, and it promises a great view of the Misty Fjords National Monument."

Colleen nodded. "It's quite breathtaking and beautiful. I've done it before but would love it if you would go."

Jess shrugged. "Why not? Sounds like a great way to take in the scenery."

Colleen smiled, a slight twinkle in her eye. "Wonderful." She opened her purse and took out a folded paper. "Here's the confirmation you can use, and George has all the details, so he'll work out any issues with the tour company."

George bent forward and craned his neck toward Jess. "We'll meet on Deck 5 at eight o'clock."

"Great, I'll be there." She met Colleen's eyes. "Thank you. That's kind of you to think of me."

Colleen asked all the men what they had done with their day and then turned to Jess. "What did you do with yourself today?"

"Not much, except I did go to the paint and sip class."

Colleen's eyes widened. "Dean, did you hear that? George and I have been telling him how popular those are. We think he should try to do that once he gets moved to Friday Harbor. Locals and tourists alike love that stuff. He's quite talented and would do a fabulous job."

Dean grinned. "Yes, Jess told me about her painting experience. I need to get settled first, but promise I'll check into it. I'll need to find a venue that has a liquor license and is open to the idea."

George waved his hand. "Oh, Jack can help you with that. He knows everybody and has tons of connections. His son Nate owns a delivery service and is bound to know somebody at one of the local spots."

Dean nodded. "I'm going to take a trip over there in a couple of weeks just to scope things out before I move in August. I want to get a feel for it and talk to Jack."

George bobbed his head. "Excellent. Then you can get the lay of the land without the stress of moving."

Colleen smiled at him. "Spend a few days enjoying yourself, and then you'll know what you need to make your new place your own. Jack and his wife will be able to tell you the best spots, and I know the building you're in is near the harbor, close to all the shops, so it will be a great location."

Dean chuckled. "You know me, Colleen. I'm pretty simple. As long as I have a bed, and there's a place for Rebel, that's all I need."

She smiled and shook her head, a bit of sheen in her eyes. "I'm going to miss you three men." She turned to Jess again. "Phil is moving near the Tri-Cities, and Doug will be up in Bellingham." She chuckled and added, "I told George we're set for a big road trip and have lots of places to visit and stay."

Dean and the other two men smiled and murmured that they would always be welcome and hoped they would plan a visit.

Despite being grown men, soldiers who had faced down many an enemy, Jess saw the trepidation in their eyes. She understood.

Change was difficult.

Change was scary.

After another delicious meal and the willpower to pass on dessert, Jess said her goodbyes. She planned to get in some exercise on the upper deck before the rain that was promised arrived.

"I did far too much sitting today and need to get in the habit of increasing my physical activity whenever I can. That's one thing that will be nice about retirement. No more excuses."

Colleen winked. "If you're anything like me, you'll just find new excuses." She patted her ample mid-section and laughed.

Jess woke at the sound of the alarm she'd set. She didn't want to risk being late for the outing, and her sleep patterns were all over the place.

After a couple of loops around the upper decks last night, she had gone to her cabin early. Despite the blackout curtains, she found it difficult to go to sleep when it was still light outside. The curtains also made the small space feel more cramped, and she would have preferred not to use them. After tossing and turning, reading, watching television, and even practicing some meditation, she finally slept.

With the upcoming plane ride, she opted to skip breakfast but indulged in a cup of tea at the café.

The group of men and the dogs arrived, and George led the way off the ship. They loaded into the shuttle and drove the short distance to the float plane tour company terminal.

The men, all experienced with flying in all types of

aircraft and in frightful conditions, stood relaxed, not a care in the world, as the staff went over all the safety protocols. As she had with the muster drill, Jess paid close attention to the overview. She hadn't been in a small plane, and her stomach fluttered when she realized just how small it was.

The pilot, Larry, who Jess guessed to be close to her age with gray hair and a kind smile, continued to talk and explained how long he had been flying, which was decades, starting with his time in the military. The company had an impeccable safety record, and there was no bad weather this morning.

She willed herself to breathe and relax, taking solace in the fact that the flight was just over an hour. She felt Rebel's snout against her leg and turned to see Dean's smile. He leaned and whispered, "He can tell you're nervous. Once you get up there, you'll be amazed by everything and forget your worries. Trust me, it'll be okay."

With the safety lecture over and all the questions answered, Larry and another staff member helped everyone load from the dock and into the plane. Their group had the plane to themselves. Dean and Rebel sat in the two seats across the aisle from Jess, who took the single seat.

Dean prepped his camera while Jess made sure her seatbelt was tight and put on the headphones. Calm, instrumental music came from them and coupled with the gentle motion of the plane atop the water, Jess relaxed.

Before she had time to worry much, the little plane skimmed along the water and lifted into the air. The pilot pointed out landmarks and flew them over the Tongass

National Forest, which Jess learned was America's largest forest at over seventeen million acres.

The lush green trees, primarily spruce, hemlock, and cedar, clung to the snow-capped mountains. Their route to Misty Fjords took them over Revillagigedo Island, in the midst of the deep blue sparkling waters. Colleen had been right. The views were nothing short of stunning.

Larry headed to Misty Fjords and true to the name, wisps of fog greeted them as they made their way between the majestic granite cliffs and lakes that looked like sapphire jewels placed at the bottom of them. He dipped a bit lower and pointed out a bear on a rocky area near a pool of water.

Larry circled the area in a gentle arc and drew their attention to a magnificent cascading waterfall spouting from the rock and disappearing into the forest. As the plane moved along the cliffs, Larry pointed out a sheer expanse where small waterfalls fell from great heights. Jess tried to count them, but there were dozens.

She gasped at the beauty and realized she could have never seen this part of Alaska, except in a plane. Jess clicked her button to talk and asked Dean if he was getting some good shots from his window.

He kept shooting and said, "Oh, yeah, this is great. What a beautiful area."

Larry's voice came through her headset. "I'm going to set it down in a few minutes, and we can get out on the shore. You can take some pictures without the window between you and all of this."

Jess gripped the armrest as Larry descended. She braced herself for the landing, but her worries were for naught. Smooth as glass, the plane glided onto the water, and Larry guided it to the shore.

He helped everyone out onto the rocky outcrop that nature provided as a makeshift dock. The dogs gravitated to the water and slurped up a drink from the pristine lake.

Jess stood, taking it in from every angle. She couldn't get enough of the awe-inspiring setting. It was like nothing she'd ever seen. The drama of the rugged mountain peaks, with green trees seeming to grow right out of them, contrasted against the calm waters in the narrow canyon below, was something she would remember forever.

She snapped several photos with her phone and took some of Dean with Rebel and the entire group with all of the men and the dogs. Larry volunteered to snap a few for her and urged her to stand with the group, with the stunning background of Misty Fjords.

Jess hated to leave the beauty and serenity of the perfect spot. The mirror-like water reflected the blue sky and clouds above, and she loved the quiet and peaceful place.

They loaded back in the plane, and Larry gave them one last look at the Misty Fjords before they turned and headed back to Ketchikan.

From the air, Jess had a new perspective on how vast Alaska was. The ports they visited were all small towns nestled along the water, but the bird's-eye view she enjoyed from the plane gave way to an expanse of land, water, and mountains, bigger than anything she had ever seen.

Once back on the ground, they thanked Larry for his expertise and made their way to the main street. Dean pointed down the road. "It's just over a mile to the dock, and the dogs need a walk. Do you feel like joining us or would you rather take the shuttle back to the ship?"

"I'm game for walking. It will be nice to be on land for a bit."

George chuckled. "The ship leaves at one o'clock, so we've got plenty of time."

The group strolled along the street, taking in the colorful buildings and shops, with the walkways filled with cruisers. Jess imagined the local economy relied heavily on the cruise ships for support.

The aroma coming from the doors of the cafés and restaurants caused Jess' stomach to growl. With the fear of getting sick on the plane behind her, breakfast sounded good. They walked at a leisurely pace, letting the dogs get some exercise and were back to the ship well before noon.

George said his goodbyes, and Phil and Doug set out on separate paths. Dean glanced at Jess. "What are you doing the rest of the day?"

She shrugged. "I hadn't given it much thought, but I'm starving, so the first order of business is a late breakfast."

"Mind if I join you?"

"Not at all." She led the way to her favorite café, and they put in their orders. The morning rush was over, and the lunch crowd hadn't arrived, so it took no time at all for their number to be called.

Dean offered to pick up their trays and returned with cheesy omelets for both of them. Between bites, he scrolled through his photos and shared some of his favorites. Along with the breathtaking waterfalls and scenery, he had a great one of Rebel sitting on top of a rocky outcrop looking quite noble at he stared out at the water.

"Oh, I love this one. That would be great framed."

He smiled. "It's a good one of him. I think some of these would make eye-catching greeting cards."

She nodded. "Oh, yes, I love using those, and you're right. They'd be popular. When you get moved, you could do that same thing around the islands and put together packets of them or postcards for people who maybe don't have time to get to everything or just want professional quality for keepsakes or cards."

He took a sip of his mocha. "I'm sort of getting excited now, just thinking about possibilities and maybe finding a shop that would be willing to carry them."

"George mentioned Jack is connected, so I think that sounds like a good start. I'm sure he knows all the business owners and if memory serves, Friday Harbor is a popular tourist destination."

He sighed. "I think it will be a good move. I'm just working myself up anticipating and worrying about things."

She took a sip from her latte. "I'm the queen of doing that, so I totally understand."

"Uh, Jess, this is going to sound really odd, and it's awkward, so I totally get it if you don't want to consider it."

Her forehead creased as she watched him struggle.

"How would you feel about going with me when I make the trip to check it out?" He didn't give her time to answer. "It's probably a dumb idea. I could use a wingman, or wing woman." He laughed. "I feel sort of connected to you. Safe, I guess."

Jess nodded as her mind raced. She wanted to say yes, but the practical part of her brain kept her from it. This is how those tragic movies started. Some lady takes off with a guy she barely knows and then wonders why she ends up killed.

What was she thinking? She considered herself a good judge of character and could pick up on a liar at fifty yards. All those years of teaching and working with so many people, and she'd rarely been wrong.

It would be nice to go somewhere and have a companion. What would people think though? What would her mom have thought if she was still here?

As she wrestled with all the what-ifs, she realized nobody would even know or care if she went with Dean. It wasn't like he was asking her to marry him, just to go with him to look at his place, as a friend. He was also in need of a companion of the human variety.

She noticed the worry in his eyes as he waited for an answer.

She took a deep breath. "I think that sounds great. I've got nothing planned and need to say yes to new things. I'd just need to find a place to stay that will take Ruby."

He smiled, relief flooding his face. "Right, right. Let me email Jack and see if he has any ideas." He pulled out his phone. "I'll do it right now while we're still here in port and have service. I probably won't know anything until tomorrow night when we get to Victoria."

"I'm looking forward to that stop. We have such a short time there, though. I thought it would probably be my favorite port, but after today and that trip, I don't think much can top it."

He finished tapping on the screen and slipped the

phone back into his pocket. "I agree, that was something I'll never forget. It makes you realize how small you are when you're in the midst of such grandeur."

Jess reached for her latte and couldn't help but admire Dean's brown eyes, noticing the gold flecks in them and the relaxed smile that filled his face. A hint of attraction tugged at her heart. She hoped she wasn't making a mistake by agreeing to accompany him.

They were just friends, she assured herself.

EIGHT

After lounging with her book for a couple of hours, Jess took a shower and changed her clothes into something more presentable for her tea date with Colleen. She made her way through the busy passageways, to the Crystal Dining Room. With the ship at sea, all the lounges and public areas were full of passengers looking for something to do to pass the time.

She found Colleen at a table for two next to a window, set with gleaming silverware atop soft-pink napkins, beautiful tea cups, and a small vase of pink and white flowers.

Colleen was decked out in a pretty camisole and glittery floral jacket. She smiled at Jess. "How was the float plane trip?"

Jess slid into the chair across from Colleen and recognized the comforting hint of lavender that accompanied the older woman. "It was awesome. I'm so glad you urged me to go. I was a little nervous, but it turned out to be my favorite thing I've done so far."

The server arrived with their tower of goodies and a pot of tea. Colleen said, "I ordered Earl Grey, so hope that's okay with you."

"Perfect," said Jess, as she watched the server pour their cups.

They nibbled on finger sandwiches and chatted about the scenery Jess had enjoyed at Misty Fjords. As she listened to Colleen, she understood why she was so good at her role in helping at Hope Foundation. Her voice and laughter could put anyone at ease. Spending time with her was like being curled up with a warm blanket. Jess felt like she was sitting across from her mom.

Jess imagined she provided a welcome soft and safe place for the men and women dealing with the wounds and scars of war. George was supportive and kind, but all about action and getting things done. Colleen focused more on the emotional well-being of everyone. Not that she was a trained therapist, but she was non-judgmental, calm, and wise.

Jess refilled their cups and selected one of the pastries. "I have an odd question for you and hope you'll give me your honest opinion. Sitting here, I almost feel like I'm chatting with my mom. I lost her earlier this year and miss her so much. She was my sounding board, and I could use her advice."

Colleen reached across the table, her wrinkly hand rubbing the top of Jess'. "I'm so sorry, dear. I still miss my mom. There's nothing that can replace that unconditional love or that special closeness."

Jess nodded. "Dean and I were visiting after we got back to the ship. He asked me if I would go with him to visit Friday Harbor when he goes over in a couple of weeks to check it out."

Colleen's eyes sparkled as she smiled. "He's such a quiet man, but I knew he trusted you, from that first night at dinner. He's also smiled more these last few days than from all the time I've known him." She took a sip of tea. "I can assure you Dean is a fine person, a true gentleman, and if you were my daughter, I'd feel quite safe for you to accompany him. He's struggled over the years, as most of the men and women in our program, but he's made huge progress. Rebel really changed him."

The tension in Jess' shoulders loosened. "He's shared some of that with me. We were talking about how scary change can be. I have some of the same worries now that I'm retired. I've had the same routine for so long and now, without Mom, I'm not sure how I'm going to handle it."

Colleen's eyes communicated her understanding. "Him trusting you is a huge step. He's reluctant too. That, and I know moving somewhere new is a challenge for him. He likes the routine he's got now, but he is more than ready for this, and we're just a phone call away. I'm sure we'll squeeze in a visit as soon as he gets settled."

Jess ran her finger across the saucer with the gold rim. "I said yes, probably not thinking it all the way through, just happy to have something to look forward to, and I think Dean could use the support. Now, I've been sort of second-guessing myself. I haven't been on anything resembling a date in years. My divorce was hard and shattered me in so many ways."

Colleen shook her head. "It sounds to me like it's well past time for you to experience something new and exciting. I bet you could use a little change of scenery and an outing. I'm sorry your divorce is still causing you such grief."

Jess reached for her tea. Her throat was suddenly dry, and she took several swallows. "Bruce, my ex, he had an affair with my best friend." She shook her head. "I should say, the woman I thought was my *best friend*. Anyway, it was awful and not only did my marriage implode, but Jake, our son, took Bruce's side, and I was the outcast. I never told Jake what Bruce had done and Bruce tried to convey it was his fault, but Jake pegged me as the cause. Losing him was worse than losing Bruce."

Colleen reached across the table again and this time gripped Jess' hand. "That had to make you feel horrible and so alone."

Jess nodded, holding back the tears burning in her eyes. "I really thought things would get better when Jake was older, but they haven't. Now, without Mom—we lived together—I feel so lost. So alone. The idea of a trip and getting to know Dean better, along with being there for him when I know he could use the support, made sense."

Colleen bobbed her head and smiled. "It still makes sense, dear. It's just hard to do something new. It's safer to stay in your own little bubble and not risk being vulnerable. But, in doing so, you miss out on so many opportunities. You deserve more, Jess. It takes courage. I know you have plenty of it, or you wouldn't have survived all you have."

Jess smiled at the sweet woman, who made her feel better with her kind words. She gazed out the window at the vast blue waters. "Honestly, I haven't felt like investing the time it takes to get to know someone new. Someone like Dean. I have these fluttery feelings I haven't had for a very long time. I'm just not sure what to make of it. I feel like I'm in unfamiliar territory. I don't want to give Dean the wrong idea since I know he's in a fragile position, too."

Colleen winked at her. "Give your brain a rest and let your heart guide you. It's rarely wrong. It's easy to get mired down in the disappointments in life. Sometimes, they are so difficult and daunting, it makes you just want to give up. Crawl in a dark hole and stay there. That's why it's so important to embrace happiness, even the possibility of happiness. Welcome the adventure with open arms. You might be surprised."

Jess let out a long breath.

Colleen gave her hand one more squeeze before letting it go. "You know, you don't have to decide everything at once. Get to know Dean and let him get to know you. At worst, you'll make a new friend, and I can tell you from experience, you won't find a more loyal one than Dean. At best, maybe you'll both find out there's something special, something more between you. There's no way to know until you take that first step."

Colleen helped herself to a scone and added, "I always say life is much too short not to spend it being happy."

Jess took a forkful of the strawberry and cream-laced square of cake. Colleen made sense, and it was true, she didn't have to have all the answers, and she needed to up her happiness game.

After indulging in their two-hour tea, there was no way Jess would be hungry for dinner. She walked back to her cabin and called Dean to let him know she was going to pass on dinner.

His calm voice came through the receiver. "I was thinking about just grabbing something quick myself. I took a look at the show in the theatre, but it didn't sound that great to me, so I was just now looking through the list of movies to see if I could find a good one."

"That's a good idea. I'm not much for a big crowd anywhere tonight. We've still got all day tomorrow at sea. I think we get to Victoria at seven o'clock. I'm going to have to take a nap so I can stay up and enjoy the few hours we have there."

Dean chuckled. "I hear ya. I'd like to make it an early night tonight, but I need to stay up late enough to take Rebel to the upper deck for some playtime." Following an awkward silence, Dean continued, "If you feel like watching a movie, you could join us."

Jess remembered Colleen's words about embracing the possibilities. "Sure, that sounds good to me. What time works?"

"How about seven thirty?"

"Perfect, I'll see you then."

Her heart pounding, she hung up the phone. Spending a few hours alone with Dean made her more nervous than the idea of a trip to Friday Harbor. She wiggled her shoulders and made a few arcs with her arms, trying to shake off the jitters.

She changed out of her nicer clothes and into something more comfortable. She didn't want him to think she thought this was a date. She opted to take a walk and distract herself instead of sitting in her cabin and worrying for two hours.

She trekked up the stairs and did a couple of laps on the exercise track before taking the stairs down to Deck 5. After checking at the concierge desk, she made her way to the café. She perused the offerings and selected a few snacks and goodies and took their warm drinks to go in a carrier, before making her way to the Baja Deck and knocking on Cabin 410.

Dean greeted her with a warm smile and took the drink carrier from her. "Wow, this is nice."

She shrugged. "It wouldn't be a movie night without some snacks, right?"

Rebel was beside Dean, his tail wagging.

"I've got a list of movies narrowed down, and I'll let you pick." Dean led her through to the sitting area. He removed her drink and handed it to her.

"Remember, I've spent the last thirty-two years with elementary kids, so my taste in movies is probably not the best."

He grinned. "I'll risk it." He handed her the list.

She studied the *Majestic Sea* notepad and his very neat printing. He had a mixture of old classics and new movies she had never heard of mixed with a few popular titles she recognized.

Her brow furrowed. "I hate to be the one to pick."

"I'm fine with any of them. I'll watch anything on the list."

She scanned the list again. "Okay, how about *Enola Holmes*? I haven't seen it and the idea of Sherlock having a sister fascinates me."

"Perfect. I haven't seen it either." He navigated to the screen and cued up the movie.

She gripped her cup tighter. "I have a confession to make. I made a reservation at The Empress in Victoria for nine thirty tomorrow. Years ago, I went to the Bengal Lounge and loved it, but they've remodeled, and it's no longer there. The concierge assured me the new lounge, Q Bar, is top notch. I snagged a spot on The Veranda. It has such a pretty view of the water, and I thought it might be fun. I wasn't sure if you had plans with George and your group or not."

"Sounds great. I don't have a real plan for tomorrow. Just figured on wandering around with Rebel, taking some photos, not much else."

She pulled a tourist guidebook from her handbag. "I picked this up, so we could figure out where to go. Being so short on time, the options are limited." She shrugged and took a seat on the couch. "The concierge recommended walking along the harbor. He said the shops and restaurants are open late, but tour-wise, there isn't much unless we want to take the bus to the gardens. Personally, I'd rather go to the gardens when I have all day."

Dean looked at the map as she talked. "It looks like it's less than a two-mile walk from the cruise terminal to the harbor. I think that's doable, don't you? We could get a taxi on the way back if need be."

She nodded. "It should be easy to get one from the Empress, and we want to be back in plenty of time."

He tilted his head toward the television. "Shall we start the show?"

She jumped from her seat and hurried to the desk

where Dean had put the takeout bag. "Don't forget our snacks." She unearthed containers of fruit, ham and cheese croissants, mini-quiches, and some cookies and cheesecake bites.

His eyes widened. "I'm glad I didn't eat dinner." They each added their selections to the paper plates included in the bag and settled onto the couch.

Jess shivered when a breeze filtered in from the open balcony door. Dean reached for the extra blanket across the top of the couch and settled it over her shoulders. "If it gets too chilly, I'll close it. Rebel likes to sit outside."

She glanced at the dog, happily sitting on his bed, looking out over the water. "I don't blame him. I'm sure the small space in the cabin gets old."

The opening credits came on the screen, and Jess snuggled under the blanket and popped a mini cheesecake in her mouth. They nibbled and sipped while they watched the engaging movie. The mystery and the characters kept Jess' interest, and each time she glanced at Dean, he was engrossed in it.

The next two hours went by quickly. By the time the movie ended, Rebel had moved indoors and was cuddled up on the couch next to Dean. Their drinks long gone and most of the snacks eaten, Jess put the few left in the box and rose from the couch. "That was pretty good."

Dean nodded, and Rebel opened his eye. "Yeah, I liked it." He sighed. "That's one thing that will be nice having my own place. I can control the television. In the group home, there's one in the main living area and in the evenings, we sometimes watch it, but it's usually tuned to sports."

"Not much on sports, huh?"

He shrugged. "I enjoy watching baseball at times, but twenty-four-seven sports is not my thing. I'd rather be outdoors anyway or working on my projects."

"Sitting in front of the television isn't healthy anyway. And I've sworn off watching the news. It's much too depressing."

Rebel stretched and raised his head. Dean ruffled the top of his head. "It's about time, buddy. You ready to go play?"

He didn't need to ask twice. At the sound of the word, he bolted off the couch, shook a little, and wandered to the door.

Dean smiled and grabbed the leash. "You feel like joining us? Should be our last night for this since tomorrow we'll get in plenty of walking."

"Sure, as long as you don't mind me stopping to get another hot tea and my heavy jacket." She rubbed her hands on her arms. "I'm chilly tonight."

"We'll walk with you." He slipped into his jacket and attached Rebel's leash.

They made a quick stop at Jess' cabin and then down to Deck 5 for hot drinks. By the time they reached the upper deck, Phil and Doug were there with their two dogs.

Rebel and Dean joined them inside the court, and the ball throwing began. Jess took advantage of the time to make several loops around the deck. As she did, her thoughts drifted to Dean and their evening spent watching a movie.

She wasn't ready to call it a date but being there next to him had felt warm and cozy. She had missed having a good friend in her life. She had let her mom fill that void left by Bruce and Jake. After the disaster with her best friend, she had sworn off getting too close to anyone. She didn't trust her judgment.

This, though, this felt different.

Dean was sincere and honest. He didn't put on airs or pretend to be something more. He had lived through and seen the worst of humanity and came out on the other side, bruised, but still alive. She was also bruised and admired his strength to move forward into the unknown.

She wasn't sure she was that brave.

NINE

Friday morning, Jess woke late in the morning. She was in no hurry to get out of bed and with the ship not arriving in Victoria until after dinner, there was no rush. After a quick shower, she went about packing her bags and getting things organized. The forecast for Victoria was clear, so she slipped her trusty red rain boots in a plastic bag and put them in her suitcase. They had served her well, but she was happy not to have to wear them again. They'd be back in Seattle in less than twenty-four hours, and she didn't want to have to pack when she got back late tonight.

She had been looking for ways to pass the time on the way to Victoria and last night, talked Dean into joining her for a game of Pub Trivia in the lounge this morning. First, she made her way to the theatre where a colorful box sat on a table outside the doors. She dropped her guess at the murderer into it. The participants had to have them in the box before noon, and the murderer would be revealed later in the afternoon at a big celebration show.

With that done, she visited the café for a delicious almond croissant and a latte, and then met Dean and Rebel in the lounge for the game. They joined in with two older couples who invited them to their table.

Estelle, the woman seated next to Jess, leaned over and said, "We're not too serious, so hopefully, you aren't either. Some of these people treat it like a profession."

Jess smiled and assured her they were just looking for a fun way to pass some time. Servers circulated and offered drinks and snacks before the host began the game. She and Dean learned the couples were related, with the women being sisters. They were experienced cruisers and had been to Alaska several times and to the Caribbean even more often.

Estelle lived in Oregon and her sister in Texas, but they and their husbands cruised together for vacations. They were dog lovers and drawn to Rebel, who relished the attention, his pink tongue hanging out of his mouth and the perpetual smile goldens seemed to have, wider. Dean and Jess didn't have time to share much about themselves before the host, with an appropriate British accent, began the game.

He whipped through twenty questions, and the six of them put their heads together to answer them. Dean's strengths were in geography and history, while Jess was most comfortable with literature and classic movies. The two couples were well rounded and versed in many topics, with both of the men excelling in sports, and their wives were masters of television shows and music.

Dean saved the day by getting the last question, knowing which European capital city was built across fourteen islands. He was the only one to know it was

Stockholm. He scribbled the answer on their sheet, right before the time was up. The host called for each table to exchange their answer sheets with the table next to them and then went through each question again.

The host was a natural entertainer, who had the crowd laughing as he encouraged them to shout out their best guesses. Their table was pleasantly surprised when they were awarded second place. Each of them received a *Majestic Star* water bottle for their efforts.

As they were leaving, Estelle said, "We'll be here again later this afternoon before dinner if you want to join us."

Jess smiled. "If we decide to come back, we'll definitely do that." She and Dean said their goodbyes and made their way to find lunch.

They opted to go to the pizza restaurant, where they were seated after a short wait. Rebel settled under their table while Jess and Dean perused the menu. Dean opted for the traditional pepperoni, and Jess chose the special majestic pizza.

They sipped iced tea while they waited for their meal. Jess sighed and said, "I've got to go to the theatre this afternoon. They're revealing the murderer in the whodunit mystery I'm playing."

Dean grinned. "I think Colleen is playing that. She's got a folder she carries with clues in it."

Jess laughed. "That's the one. I think I have it figured out but could have used another clue."

"Is there a big prize for the winner?"

Jess shook her head. "I doubt it. I think there will be several of us who get it right, and then there's a raffle, so only one prize winner."

He held up his water bottle. "Maybe a towel or robe to

go with this?"

She grinned. "Probably. I did it more for the fun of it. I'm not sure they even said what the prize was. I've always wanted to go to one of those murder mystery dinners and thought this was my chance."

The waiter brought out their pizzas, each a personal size, and they dug into them. The melted cheese and herbs mingled in her mouth, and she raised her brows at Dean. "Mine is really good, better than I expected. How's yours?"

He nodded and reached for another slice. "It's great. I figured it would be more like the chains, but this is better, more like those wood-fired places."

As they ate, they chatted about Victoria. She took another piece from the pan, freeing the long string of cheese with her fork, and set it on her plate. "I really wish we had more time and that we were there earlier in the day. It would have been fun to tour the Parliament Building and go to the museum, not to mention the gardens and tea at the Empress."

Dean took a long swallow of his iced tea. "You know, I checked on the ferry from Friday Harbor over to Victoria. It only takes about an hour. Maybe we could go for the day when you come with me to check out the place. We could make it a really long day and see the gardens, along with anything else."

His suggestion warmed her heart. She couldn't remember the last time Bruce had put forth any effort to think of something special she wanted to do. The gardens were probably not high on Dean's list, but he was willing to make a special trip so she could see them.

She smiled and ran her finger along the edge of the

pizza pan. "That's so nice of you to think of that. I would love to go to the gardens. I hope you wouldn't be too bored."

He grinned, and her heart fluttered. She liked seeing him smile. It revealed an almost boyish innocence to his otherwise serious demeanor. Colleen had noticed him smiling more, and a tiny part of Jess liked the thought that it was because of her.

"Nah, I think I could get some great photos. When we talked about postcards and greeting cards, I was thinking flowers would be popular and what better place, right?"

She nodded. "Oh, yes. I think that would be terrific. How many days are you planning on for your visit?"

He shrugged. "I'm flexible. I thought a couple of days, but I'm open to whatever."

"I think it might take more than one day to see everything."

Rebel came from under the table and sat next to Dean. He reached and petted the top of the dog's head. "You could always come back for another visit."

She reached for her iced tea. "True. I'm going to be footloose and fancy free. It's going to take some time to adjust to all this freedom."

He rested his hand atop Rebel's head. "I'm a little intimidated to leave my routine behind. It'll take me some time to get in the groove of a new place and a new job."

"I bet you'll enjoy it. I think it's a pretty slow pace over there, especially once the tourist season is over."

"I'm not a fan of big crowds, so that sounds good to me."

She nodded. "I hear ya. Where I live on Mercer Island, it's changed over the last few years. Lots more people and traffic than there used to be. Or maybe I'm just getting old."

That made him smile again.

After lunch, they detoured to Dean's cabin, and he picked up his camera. Then, they strolled along the upper deck. The sun was shining, and it made for a wonderful view as the ship moved among the islands and coastline as it made its way to Vancouver Island.

They, along with several other passengers, enjoyed the warmth of the sun and the picture-perfect views. As the time neared for Jess to attend the mystery reveal show, they made plans to meet up for a snack before the ship docked.

Dean and Rebel left her when the elevator arrived at the Baja Deck. "I need to get everything packed up," he said, guiding Rebel through the doors. "I'll see you at the café."

"Sounds good. I'll be there."

She took the elevator the rest of the way and along the Promenade Deck until she reached the theatre. Several passengers were making their way through the doors. She turned at the sound of her name.

Colleen was several feet away from her, waving.

Jess walked toward her and smiled. "Dean thought you'd be here. I'm so glad you saw me."

"Oh, yes. I can hardly wait to find out who the culprit is." She led the way to seats a few rows down. As soon as they were seated, she leaned over to Jess and whispered, "I guessed it was the co-star."

Jess chuckled. "She was my guess as well. All the clues pointed to her."

Colleen nodded. "And she's quite full of herself, isn't she?"

Soon, the entire cast of characters, from the gaffer and camera operator to the writer and critic, along with the movie actors and actresses, took the stage. The costumes were wonderful, and they all did a great job playing their parts. The director served as the narrator and outlined his own demise, teasing the audience with who the guilty party could have been.

He finally revealed the person who poisoned him was indeed the co-star, who was wearing a very skimpy evening gown and protesting her innocence.

The crowd erupted in applause at the end of the presentation, and the director asked everyone in the audience who had guessed correctly to stand.

Colleen and Jess joined the hordes of people who stood as the director pointed to one of the colorful boxes they had used to dispense clues. All the correct answer sheets were in the box, and he was about to pull the winner.

Dramatic music played while he shook the box, then opened the lid and pulled an entry form. A drumroll led up to his announcement of a woman who squealed with delight when her name was called.

They brought her up on stage and presented her with a new tablet and a tote bag full of *Majestic Star* swag. She was ecstatic and reminded Jess of those old game shows when the winners would jump around and scream.

She and Colleen turned to each other and shrugged.

"Oh, well," said Colleen. "I already have a tablet and don't need any more junk."

"Same for me," Jess said as they stood.

As they made their way to the doors of the theatre, Colleen asked, "Do you have time to join me for a glass of wine?"

"I've got time but will probably go for tea or something soft."

"Oh, of course, anything you like." She led the way to the wine bar she and George liked.

The staff greeted Colleen like an old friend and brought her a glass of Merlot without even asking. Jess ordered an Arnold Palmer.

Jess took a long swallow from her glass and asked, "What are you and George going to do in Victoria?"

Colleen took another sip of wine. "Oh, we're meeting some friends who live on Vancouver Island for dinner. They live in Parksville, so it's about a two-hour drive for them. They got a room and are going to stay overnight so they don't have to worry about driving home."

"That sounds fun."

"And what about you? Do you and Dean have plans?"

Jess felt the heat crawl up her neck and settle in her cheeks. "I booked us a table on The Veranda at The Empress later tonight. Other than that, we decided to walk from the dock to the harbor and just take in the sights and maybe duck into any shops that look interesting."

"With it being so late, it's hard to plan anything."

"Dean and I were talking about it today, and he suggested when we make the trip to Friday Harbor, we take the ferry over so I can go to the gardens."

"Oh, that's a wonderful idea. You should get quite the show with the roses in bloom."

Jess took another sip and sighed. "We were talking about Dean's new job, and we came up with the idea of him creating some postcards and greeting cards with his photos. Maybe get one of the local shops to carry them. He liked that idea and thought he could get some great florals there."

Colleen's eyes twinkled with delight. "You are so good for him. That is terrific, and I'm sure Jack could help him find a shop willing to do that. They get so many tourists, and they would snap those up."

"I think so, too." She glanced out the window. "I'm looking forward to the trip. I'm surprised in a way. I didn't even want to come on this cruise, but like you said, I need to be open to new experiences."

Colleen patted her hand. "Exactly, dear. Instead of saying no to things, try to focus on the idea of *why not*. You've got your whole life ahead of you; you're retired and free to do anything you like."

"I'm hoping I can reconnect with my son and spend time with him. I'm fearful because the rejection hurts so much."

Colleen's smile faded. "There's no easy answer for that. Over the years of working with our veterans, I've seen so much hurt between families. Like you said, the rejection, especially from those we love most, is heartbreaking. My best advice is to just let him know you love him and that you want to see him. Make it easy, try not to guilt him, and leave the door wide open. Often, it takes much longer than we want, but in their own time, they come back to us."

Colleen let out a long breath. "In the meantime, live your life. Don't worry it away waiting for the day when all will be right with the world. It may never be right, then you'll have squandered the gift of time. When you're old, like me, you realize it's the little things in life that mean the most. You'll regret not doing things you wanted to do when you were able. The body eventually wears out, and you just can't do what you thought you could. So, don't waste too much time fretting about the past or what you've lost. Focus all your energy on what you have and making the most of it."

After spending the time with Colleen, Jess understood why Dean was reluctant to leave the program. Being near her, you couldn't help but feel better. She inspired confidence and made everything seem doable. She would have made an excellent teacher.

Jess finished her drink and hugged Colleen goodbye. "I need to get back to my cabin. I'm not sure I'll see you before we dock tomorrow. I sure hope I get to see you again. It's been such a pleasure."

Colleen slipped a finger into the pocket on her lanyard and pulled out a business card. "You call me anytime, and you're welcome to visit." She hugged Jess in a tight embrace. "I have a feeling I'll see you again."

Jess held back tears as she hugged her again. The waiter delivered another glass of wine as Jess waved goodbye to the woman she felt like she'd known much longer than a week.

Jess ran her fingers over the business card in her palm. She vowed to keep in touch, if only by phone or email, but hoped to see her again.

TEN

After a light snack and tea at the café, Jess and Dean, along with his furry sidekick, made their way to disembark. Once off the ship, they followed St. Lawrence until they reached the pathway that ran along the water.

With an impeccable view, they took their time traveling the walkway that ran behind restaurants and hotels. A few boats were in the harbor, but the cute little water taxis Jess remembered from a long-ago trip were done for the night. That was another thing she wanted to be sure to do when they came back for a visit to the gardens.

Dean's phone pinged a few times, and they stopped while he dug it out of his pocket. Now with cell service, his messages and emails were coming through. The notifications prompted her to put in a call to Carly. She was dying to see her sweet Ruby.

Carly's smiling face filled the little screen and after a quick chat, she maneuvered Ruby into view. Jess talked to her sweet girl and watched her ears perk. Her brown eyes glistened with excitement as Jess kept talking. Dean stuck his head closer to Jess and said, "Oh, she's gorgeous. I can't wait to meet her in person."

Jess talked for a few more minutes and assured Ruby she'd see her in the morning. She thanked Carly and signed off, reaching to pet the top of Rebel's head. She had missed Ruby so much and couldn't wait to let her snuggle on her lap.

Dean tapped on the screen of his phone and turned to Jess. "Jack says my apartment won't be ready when we come to visit, so I need a place to stay, too. He's got two options that would work for us. Both are friends of Jack and close friends of his son Nate. The first one is Sam, who owns the local coffee shop, and her husband Jeff. They have a place on the water and would love to have us. They have two guest rooms and a golden retriever, plus a chocolate Labrador."

He looked at Rebel, who raised his eyebrows at the mention of the dogs, and Dean smiled at him. "I think he understands every word I say." His eyes returned to his phone. "Linda, who owns the nursery and is a florist, and her husband, Max, have a place with plenty of room, and they have a black Labrador. Jack added that Nate and his wife also have a golden retriever. They're all excited to meet me and you and since we'll be there around the Fourth of July, they encouraged us to stay for the big celebration. Sounds like there are six couples who get together, and they're all dog owners with several goldens in the mix."

"Wow, that's so nice. I didn't expect to stay with anyone. I figured Jack would recommend a motel or something."

Dean nodded. "Jack has been terrific, and I know he's trying to make me feel at home. Honestly, the apartment is probably fine, but I know he wants it all ship-shape before I stay in it. They were doing some refurbishing."

"I love the idea of staying with people who have dogs. That would be great, but I don't want to impose."

Dean chuckled. "I'm sure if it were an imposition, Jack wouldn't have suggested it. I think he's like Colleen and George. One of the good people in the world and like George said, he knows everyone on the island. Maybe this won't be such an adjustment. It'll be nice to get to know them before I show up in August. They want to show us around and are planning an outdoor party to welcome us."

Her heart filled with gratitude as she watched Dean's face relax. She knew he was worried about the move but hearing the excitement in his voice and seeing some of the strain disappear made her understand the depth of his concern. She was happy she'd be with him and get to meet what sounded like a wonderful community. "Wow, that sounds so nice. It doesn't matter which couple we stay with. They both sound great. I guarantee we'll have to visit the nursery you mentioned, along with the coffee shop."

Dean tapped in a reply and then put the phone in his pocket. "I told him that sounded good, and we'd stay at either place, whatever worked the best for two dogs. Or we could split up."

With that done, they continued their walk, taking in the gorgeous water and the iconic Empress Hotel that sat at the mouth of the Inner Harbour. The path took them to Bellville Street, and they passed by several hotels and the

Bateman Gallery, that had been the steamship terminal years ago.

They took the stairs down to the water level and marveled at the famous *Welcome to Victoria* sign spelled out in colorful flowers along the harbor wall. Dean took a few shots of it and made Jess pose for a few. He pointed across the water. "I'll go over that way and get some better ones."

They wandered across to the other side, and he took as many photos as possible before the sky began to fade. The huge Parliament Building, with its massive copper domes and stately grounds, made for a beautiful photo opportunity.

The turn-of-the-century style lampposts with the globe lights that dotted the sidewalks were graced with colorful baskets of flowers that hung from the top of each of them. Flowers burst from beds along the harbor and in front of the Parliament Building. Everywhere Jess looked, she gasped at the beauty and understood why Victoria was known as the City of Gardens.

Dean wanted to wait until it was darker and come back to get more shots of the lights of the Parliament Building. They wandered down Government Street, enjoying the wonderful scent of the flowers drifting through the air and the cheerful vibe and smiles from fellow tourists. Rebel was quite popular and elicited tons of praise, but Dean had added his PLEASE DON'T PET signs to his vest to help him focus and to keep people from rushing up to him.

It didn't take Jess long to find a tea shop and while Dean and Rebel waited outside, she darted through the door. Along with displays of beautiful teaware and tins of tea, they had a huge pastry counter with sinful-looking treats and savory sandwiches.

The shop smelled wonderful and inviting, and Jess could have parked herself at a table and spent hours in the place, just soaking it all in. She made her way around the displays and was tempted to buy some of the loose-leaf teas they sold by the ounce, but instead, selected several of the more practical tins of tea.

She added a gorgeous mug with a pen and ink drawing of Victoria landmarks covering it. She held it and knew it would always remind her of this fun trip. With her purchase bagged up, she left without succumbing to one of the chocolate treats that kept winking at her from the counter.

Dean had found a bench, and Rebel was resting at his feet. He greeted her with a smile. "There's a chocolate shop just down the street. Shall we check it out?"

She laughed. "I thought you'd never ask."

He offered her his arm, and they strolled along the street until they reached the small shop. As soon as Dean opened the door, the inviting aroma beckoned them. She selected a box to take to Carly as a special treat for taking such good care of Ruby. She also chose a small box for herself and happily took the sample the clerk offered her.

Dean selected a couple of pieces and took them in a bag to enjoy as they walked.

By the time he took more photos of the Parliament Building and captured several of the horse-drawn carriages, the sun was setting. They stood at the mouth of the harbor in awe, as they were treated to a stunner. The orange sky reflected across the water and above the gold slices surrounding the setting sun, was a layer of puffy clouds in smoky purple, with a bright pink underbelly.

Dean was overjoyed to capture such a beautiful night and as they turned, he took a few more of The Empress, all decked out in her white lights with her ivy-covered facade. The tree trunks were wrapped in hundreds of tiny lights twinkling in the shrubs around the entrance. "This is truly a photographer's dream," he said, as they waited to cross the street.

They climbed the steps and entered the lobby. Jess stopped and stood in awe.

The property had been renovated since she had been there years ago. She remembered the chocolate chip cookies at the registration counter and the old-fashioned feel but wasn't prepared for the modern elegance that stood in its place.

The rich gold, gray, and lavender color palette was calming and classy. The huge crystal chandelier that hung in the middle of the now opened space that gave way to the second floor and the beautiful staircase she remembered having to walk down a hallway to find before, demanded her attention.

The chandelier resembling the open petals of a flower reflected in the surrounding mirrors, making it seem even larger.

In a word, it was breathtaking.

They stepped forward across the marble-looking tile floor, and her feet sank into the thick lavender rug embedded with a gold design. They made their way up the staircase and passed by Q Bar and Q Restaurant to take a look at the tea lounge. It had also been modernized and looked so inviting with touches of purple and gray in the lighter-feeling space. It was now used in the evening for a lounge, instead of just for afternoon tea.

After admiring the new space, they went back to check in for their reservation on The Veranda. The friendly hostess led them to the outdoor space and a table with a wonderful view of the water. They walked by a table with a built-in fire pit, where guests were roasting marshmallows. The flicker of candles on each table and the warm glow from the lights above the terrace made it all the more inviting.

The hostess smiled at Rebel. "We'd be happy to bring your dog a bowl of water."

Dean settled him next to the stone wall where glass panels had been installed above it and provided an unobstructed view from their perch. "That would be great, thank you."

They perused the menu, and Dean stood at the glass wall and captured a few more fantastic shots of the sunset over the harbor waters.

"I was going to settle for a snack, but I cannot resist grilled cheese and tomato soup, so I'm going to have that," said Jess, setting her menu at the edge of the table.

Dean grinned and said, "I'm hungrier than I should be. Must be all that walking, right? The fish and chips and the burger are calling my name. I can't decide."

A young man arrived with waters for them and a big bowl of cold water for Rebel. Soon, the server appeared and took their orders, with Dean settling on fish and chips, and Jess adding a glass of Chardonnay to her order.

Colorful baskets of flowers decorated the patio area and gave them a perfect spot for taking in the focal point of the Inner Harbour and people watching to their hearts' content.

Her wine and his iced tea were delivered with a promise that their entrée would be out shortly. Jess glanced over at Dean, his shoulders relaxed with his back against the chair, focused on the scene in front of them. He looked much more at ease than the first night she met him at the railing. "Penny for your thoughts," she said.

He grinned at her—the grin that made her heart skip a beat. "Not many thoughts at all, which is unusual. This has been a great evening. One of the best I can remember. It's stunning here, and I think you're right about the move being a treasure trove for photography. I'm sort of getting more excited about it."

"That's terrific. Visually, I think it's quite similar to where you'll be, although much less populated than here."

He took a drink of his iced tea. "I'm fine with less people. I prefer it, in fact."

"Me, too," she said and reached for her wine. "However, this weather, the view, this place... I could sit here forever."

"I've never been here, but now, I can't wait to come back." His gaze met hers. "I'm really happy you're coming with me. I'm not sure I would have enjoyed the cruise without you. I haven't been around many women, outside of Colleen and the other veterans, and it's been nice... more than nice, to spend time with you."

She smiled. "I feel the same way. Since my divorce, I've really poured everything into my work and my mom. My marriage dissolving really did a number on me." She paused and added, "I didn't tell you before, but Bruce had an affair with my best friend. More than that, being estranged from my son, shattered my heart. I tried to fill those voids and numb the pain with my students and my mom. It worked for years. Until now, when both of those things are gone."

He reached for her hand and passed her a napkin.

She hadn't noticed the tears on her cheeks.

"Jess, I'm truly sorry about your loss. I can assure you, your ex-husband is an… well, let's just say imbecile. I can't imagine letting you go. For him to allow your son to blame you is really the lowest of the low."

She sighed. "I never told Jake what Bruce did, and Bruce said he tried to explain that it was his fault, but he never divulged his transgression either. I didn't want Jake to hate his father, and I don't think he hates me, but he harbors some resentment and thinks I could have kept the family together." She let go of Dean's hand and rubbed the hem of the napkin. "I probably could have stayed with Bruce, but I knew in my heart I couldn't. I couldn't trust him, and I thought the constant tension would have been worse on everyone."

"You don't have anything to feel guilty over. Colleen always says people do their best with what they have to work with, and I think you were doing your best in light of the situation. I hope Jake figures that out one day soon and reaches out to you." He took another swallow of his tea. "One of my biggest regrets is not having a child. I would give anything to have a son and can only imagine your pain in not having him in your life."

The remorse was heavy in his voice, and Jess' throat was too dry to speak.

The server chose that moment to deliver their meals. Everything looked and smelled delicious. Jess didn't waste a moment digging into her bowl of creamy soup laced with fresh basil.

Paired with the delicious mixture of melted cheese on the perfectly toasted bread, eating it was like stepping back in time. She had enjoyed the same meal, although in a much plainer style, at her mother's table too many times to count. Granted, the glass of Chardonnay was a new addition, but otherwise, it brought back fond memories.

"How's the fish and chips?"

"Delicious," said Dean, offering her a fry.

She shook her head. "I've got more than enough here."

Dean pointed across the street to the Parliament Building. "It's getting dark enough, I'll be able to get some great photos of it on our way back to the ship."

She glanced at her watch. "If we want to walk, I figure we better get going by eleven, just so we aren't late."

"Although, if I had to be stranded someplace, I wouldn't mind staying here." He wiggled his brows as he stretched out his legs.

"I'm with you on that one. I always dreamed of being locked in a library or bookstore, and this might even be better." She took her last sip of wine and sighed. "This has been a lovely trip. I was dreading it, but I've had a great time. The only thing I'm missing is my Ruby."

Dean reached down to pet Rebel. "I feel for you. I would be lost without this guy by my side."

"We need to introduce them before the trip to San Juan Island. Maybe you two could come over for dinner one evening. I'm not sure how far away you are?"

"I'm in Renton, so not too far from Mercer Island. We'd love to come over. We could come up with a game plan for the trip." He looked at Rebel and added, "Wouldn't we, boy? You'd like to meet Ruby."

His tail thumped several times and made Jess laugh.

The server brought their bill and as much as Jess protested, Dean insisted on treating. She shook her head. "Well, now you have to come to dinner for sure." She dug out her phone and tapped on the screen. Moments later, his phone chimed. "There, I've texted you my address. Let's plan on next week. Whatever day works for you."

His charming grin appeared again. "My calendar is wide open."

ELEVEN

After leaving the beautiful hotel and capturing more photos of it and the massive Parliament Building, looking magnificent with its silhouette outlined in white lights, they set out on Belleville Street, toward the cruise ship dock.

As they left the street and took the pathway along the harbor, Dean slipped his hand in Jess'. She intertwined her fingers in his. It was the best feeling in the world to know you weren't alone. While Jess hadn't thought she missed anything after her divorce and all her years with her mother, she couldn't deny the pleasure it gave her to have Dean by her side, his warm hand in hers.

She could have done everything they did today on her own, but it made it all the more special to share and enjoy the experience with Dean. The pathway was lined with the glow of soft lights and bordered by lush greenery and fragrant flowers the entire way. Boats dotted the harbor, and the view of the lights from the buildings along the waterfront reflected in the dark and calm water.

As they walked, Dean said, "Having not cruised before, I'm not sure how hectic the disembarking process is. We've got a van coming to pick up our group, so I won't have much time in the morning. George and Colleen will have a plan and a schedule."

"I've got a neighbor coming to pick me up, too. Like you, I'm not sure how it will work, but I imagine getting thousands of people off the ship will be chaotic. How about we just plan to talk tonight. That way we won't have to worry about finding each other in the crowd? We can decide on the best day for dinner later this week and firm up plans for our trip. I wouldn't mind getting the dogs together more than once, just so they're used to each other."

"That's a good idea. I've got an open week, so we could set something up, maybe meet at a park."

"Ruby's never met a dog or a person she doesn't like, but I hate to throw them together without them spending a little time playing."

"Rebel has a calm personality and has mostly been around Ace and River, but he also loves people. I'm sure they'll be great together. You know goldens."

She nodded. She couldn't wait to see her golden girl but was surprised she hadn't dwelled on her absence these last few days.

A sense of sadness came over Jess as they left the path and made their way to the ship. The escape from reality was almost over. There hadn't been enough hours in the day to suit her. They joined a steady stream of passengers who were reboarding. She noticed Dean was limping slightly. "Did you hurt your leg?"

He patted his thigh. "Old injury. I think I just overused it today. It's nothing, really."

As they entered The Atrium, Dean squeezed her hand. "How about we grab a couple of hot drinks and head up to the upper deck. We can get one last glimpse as we set sail."

It was late, and her first thought was she should get some sleep. They'd be arriving in less than seven hours.

Almost as if he saw the wheels turning in her head, Dean added, "You can sleep tomorrow. How many times have you sailed from Victoria on a night like this one?"

He had a point. "I'd love that. I just need to stop by my cabin and grab a wrap."

He nodded. "I'll get the drinks and meet you up there. I'll try to snag us a good spot before it gets too busy."

She hurried to the elevator, dashed into her room, and opened her suitcase where she had placed the beautiful wrap her mom had given her on the last Christmas she was still able to shop. It was a dark blue-green that always reminded Jess of the sea, and her mom thought it brought out her hazel eyes. She left her backpack with her purchases and tucked the wrap around her shoulders, checking her pocket to make sure she had her phone for any photo ops.

There were several passengers on the upper deck, but not as many as she thought would be there. She found Dean and Rebel at a prime spot at a table near the aft of the ship.

She slipped into the chair next to Dean and cupped her hands around the latte he had brought for her. From here, they had a view of the entire city.

Jess looked up at the night sky, filled with twinkling stars. "It's a gorgeous night."

He didn't look up but focused on her. "I agree and one I'll always remember."

The ship began to move, inching its way through the waters between Vancouver Island and the mainland. The views would have been spectacular in daylight, but Jess had no problem settling for the romance of a night voyage and the view of the lights glowing among the land masses.

As the ship drifted further away, passengers left the deck in search of a few hours of sleep in their cabins. Soon, they were alone.

Dean sighed and reached for her hand. "I meant what I said before. Meeting you, getting to know you, it's been the highlight of the cruise for me. I admit, I'm more than a little rusty when it comes to relationships, much less dating, but being with you is easy." He laughed and added, "When Colleen and George twisted my arm to come on this cruise, I never imagined meeting someone like you or having so much fun. I haven't had a panic attack since that first night when you rescued me."

She smiled and leaned her head closer to him. "I was thinking the same thing. I pictured myself miserable, nauseated, and staying in my cabin to keep my panic attacks at bay. It's been quite the surprise for me, too. A very welcome and pleasant surprise."

She took a sip from her cup. "To be honest, I was feeling awkward about agreeing to go with you to Friday Harbor. I mean, I hardly know you. It's so out of character for me, but I visited with Colleen, and she helped me understand I need to embrace life a bit more. With what you learned from Jack and the idea of seeing your new place and meeting the group of friends who seem so kind and welcoming, I'm more excited about it."

He smiled and let go of her hand, slipping his arm around her shoulder. "I had a similar conversation with George. I was feeling guilty that I had come across way too forward and probably scared you. I just don't want all of this to end, and I feel so at ease with you, more than I have in years. It would really mean so much to me to have you there. It's hard to do new things on your own but having a friend by your side makes it easy."

He started to reach for his cup and added, "It doesn't hurt that my new friend is kind and beautiful and loves my dog." He took a long swallow. "I hate to admit it, but I'm in uncharted waters here."

Thankful for the cover of darkness, she felt the bloom of heat in her cheeks. It had been years since a man had referred to her as beautiful. She leaned her head against his shoulder and gazed at the sky. "I see what you did there." She chuckled. "As a lover of words, I appreciate the reference to uncharted waters and can tell you I feel the same way. I'm not sure what this is, but I like it."

He squeezed her closer and kissed her forehead. She inhaled the spicy scent along his neck, as a tingle of electricity zipped through her. "I'm not sure either, but I'm going to take George's advice and go with it. The prospect of a new relationship thrills me and terrifies me at the same time."

She laughed. "I know exactly what you mean, but I'm not willing to pass up on the possibility of happiness. Colleen helped me realize I deserve it."

As she watched the glimmer of stars in the sky, her thoughts drifted to her mom. They had enjoyed sitting outside, stargazing. She wondered what she would think of Dean and of her daughter agreeing to go on a trip with him.

She pondered more, and one star caught her eye. It shined brighter and twinkled more than the others. She sighed and reached to pull the wrap closer to her neck. Her heart felt lighter, surer, as she continued to watch the star.

Maybe it was a sign. Just a little nudge from her mom, letting her know she approved.

Jess wanted to believe it and as she snuggled a little closer, she felt Dean's head next to hers. They may both be in uncharted waters, but she couldn't think of anyone else she'd rather be next to as they navigated their path home.

EPILOGUE

June 30th

Ruby, her green bandana covered in watermelons, followed Jess through the house. The golden retriever had scattered her toys as far away as the living room, and as Jess tossed the pink squeaky pig and orange alligator toy that the dog loved into a tote bag, Ruby's thick golden tail swished back and forth.

"You're a rascal," Jess said, and smiled. She'd put the toys in the bag earlier, but Ruby had absconded with them, running through the house with excitement. "You know something's up, don't you?"

Jess carried the tote bag back to the front door, then looked through everything inside. Dean was going to arrive soon and she didn't want to forget anything.

She counted on her fingers as she went through the bag. Food and treats, bottles of water, travel bowls, and a spare bandana since Ruby had taken a liking to wearing them. Toys, balls, and her favorite chew bones rounded out the dog tote bag.

Jess' suitcase and a tote bag full of odds and ends, plus a shopping bag of snacks was stacked next to Ruby's bed. She was glad Dean had a full-sized SUV. As she thought of Dean, doubt crept over her. She knelt down and hugged Ruby's neck. "Do you think I'm crazy, Ruby? We're going off on a trip with a guy I barely know. It's so not like me. I can't figure out if I'm excited or nuts."

Moments later, Ruby announced his arrival with lots of wiggles and frantic tail-wagging. Before he could ring the bell, Jess opened the front door.

"Good morning," he said, bending down to give Ruby a scratch behind her ears. His warm smile reached all the way to his dark brown eyes. His jacket matched his steely gray hair, styled in a close trim, that while longer and more stylish, had to have been inspired by all his years in the military. He eyed the stack of belongings. "Looks like you're ready to go."

Jess laughed. "I sure hope so. If I had more, you'd need to rent a trailer."

With no complaints, he packed all their stuff into the back of his SUV. Jess attached Ruby's leash to her harness, and with one more glance around her house, she slung her purse over her shoulder and locked the door behind her.

Carly, who lived next door with her parents, would pick up her mail and check on the house, and had even promised to water her pots of flowers. Jess couldn't think of anything else, but naturally, had a nagging feeling she was forgetting something.

She handed Dean the leash and he loaded Ruby into the backseat with Rebel, his own golden retriever, who was outfitted in his official service dog vest. The two had only met twice, but were already fast friends. They snuggled closer together, licking each other's faces.

After opening Jess' door for her and handing her their bag of snacks for the road, Dean slid behind the wheel. They had a reservation on the nine-thirty ferry and had agreed to leave at six, just to be safe. Traffic around Seattle was always heavy and they wanted to allow plenty of time to get to the ferry dock in Anacortes.

The dogs settled down next to each other as Dean entered the freeway. Stop and go traffic continued for some time, and when they finally broke free of the worst of it after Marysville, Jess felt her shoulders relax.

They arrived in Anacortes in plenty of time, and Dean pulled into a parking spot in front of a coffee shop. "Shall we grab something hot to drink and let these two out for some water and a break while we wait?"

"Sounds good. I'll get us lattes and catch up with you, if you want to handle the two hooligans."

Dean took a firm hold of the leashes before letting Rebel and Ruby out, then led them to a grassy area across the street.

Jess couldn't resist the giant cookie by the register and added it to the two drinks. She found Dean sitting on a bench, holding the leashes, while the two dogs investigated a suspicious bush next to him.

She handed him his latte and unwrapped the cookie. "Fresh from the oven. It's one of my weaknesses."

He laughed and took his half, along with a sip from his

cup. "We should be right on time to get in line, once we're done here."

She rested her back against the bench and gazed at the cotton candy sky. The soft pinks, lavenders, and blues reflected in the peaceful water that they'd soon be sailing. Her stomach did a little flip. She was excited to see where Dean would be living and working, and was looking forward to meeting Sam and Jeff, whose home they would be staying in while on San Juan Island.

Part of her was also apprehensive. Having Dean in her life these last couple of weeks had filled her days with new excitement and the anticipation of this trip. Knowing he'd be moving in August filled her with trepidation. The last thing she wanted was to get attached to someone who would soon be gone. She'd had her share of people leaving her and wasn't sure if she could handle another blow.

"We should get going," Dean said, interrupting her thoughts. Jess collected their travel bowls and followed the three of them to the SUV. Was she already too attached to Dean? As much as she wanted to see where this went, she had to be careful.

Read more about Jess and Dean in FOLLOW ME HOME, and if you haven't yet started the Hometown Harbor Series, FINDING HOME is the first book in the series.

If you enjoyed sailing away with Jess Clark on the Majestic Sea, you'll love cruising with Addison to the

Mexican Riviera in A NOT SO DISTANT SHORE, by Ev Bishop.

★ Don't miss a Sail Away book! ★

Book 1: Welcome Aboard – prologue book
Book 2: The Sound of the Sea by Jessie Newton
Book 3: Uncharted Waters by Tammy L. Grace
Book 4: A Not So Distant Shore by Ev Bishop
Book 5: Caroline, Adrift by Kay Bratt
Book 6: Moonlight on the Lido Deck by Violet Howe
Book 7: The Winning Tickets by Judith Keim
Book 8: Lost At Sea by Patricia Sands
Book 9: The Last Port of Call by Elizabeth Bromke

ACKNOWLEDGMENTS

Writing this one has been a fun adventure, especially since I've never been on a cruise! I fell in love with Jess and Ruby and while writing it, decided she needed to have her own story in my Hometown Harbor Series. FOLLOW ME HOME is the seventh book in that series and focuses on Jess' story.

I had fun teasing a trip to Friday Harbor in this one and mentioning some of my beloved characters from my Hometown Harbor Series. If you've read them, you'll recognize them, but if you're new, it will give you a glimpse into the characters I've come to think of as friends in that series, and I hope you'll try them.

My thanks to my editor, Susan, for finding my mistakes and helping me polish *Uncharted Waters*. This cover and all the covers in our Sail Away Series are gorgeous and so inviting. All the credit goes to Elizabeth Mackey for creating such beautiful covers for us. I'm fortunate to have such an incredible team helping me.

It's also fun to write a project with other authors and those in this series are among my favorites. I hope you'll read them all and enjoy your escape with each one of them.

I so appreciate all of the readers who have taken the time to tell their friends about my work and provide reviews of my books. These reviews are especially important in promoting future books, so if you enjoy my novels, please consider leaving a review. I also encourage you to follow me on major book retailers, Goodreads, and BookBub, where leaving a review is even easier, and you'll be the first to know about new releases and deals.

Remember to visit my website at http://www.tammylgrace.com and join my mailing list for my exclusive group of readers. I also have a fun Book Buddies Facebook Group. That's the best place to find me and get a chance to participate in my giveaways. Join my Facebook group at https://www.facebook.com/groups/AuthorTammyLGraceBookBuddies/
and keep in touch—I'd love to hear from you.

Happy Reading,

Tammy

FROM THE AUTHOR

Thank you for reading UNCHARTED WATERS. Writing this one felt like a vacation and makes me want to visit all these ports of call. You can read more about Jess and Dean in FOLLOW ME HOME, the seventh book in my HOMETOWN HARBOR SERIES.

If you enjoy women's fiction and haven't yet read my HOMETOWN HARBOR SERIES, I think you'll enjoy them. It's a seven-book series, with each book focused on a different female heroine. They are set in the gorgeous San Juan Islands in the Pacific Northwest, and you'll recognize some of them from their mention in UNCHARTED WATERS. You can start the series with a free prequel that is in the form of excerpts from Sam's journal. She's the main character in the first book, FINDING HOME.

I'm also excited about a brand-new women's fiction series I'm writing for 2023. It's the SISTERS OF THE HEART SERIES, set in southern Oregon and is focused on five foster girls, now grown women in mid-life and the

FROM THE AUTHOR

woman who welcomed them into her heart and home years ago. The first book, GREETINGS FROM LAVENDER VALLEY, will introduce you to all the women.

If you're a new reader and enjoy mysteries, I write a series that features a lovable private detective, Coop, and his faithful golden retriever, Gus. If you like whodunits that will keep you guessing until the end, you'll enjoy the COOPER HARRINGTON DETECTIVE NOVELS.

The two books I've written as Casey Wilson, A DOG'S HOPE and A DOG'S CHANCE have received enthusiastic support from my readers and if you're a dog lover, are must reads.

If you enjoy holiday stories, be sure and check out my CHRISTMAS IN SILVER FALLS SERIES and HOMETOWN CHRISTMAS SERIES. They are small-town Christmas stories of hope, friendship, and family. You won't want to miss any of the SOUL SISTERS AT CEDAR MOUNTAIN LODGE BOOKS. It's a connected Christmas series I wrote with four author friends. My contributions; CHRISTMAS WISHES, CHRISTMAS SURPRISES, and CHRISTMAS SHELTER. All heartwarming, small-town holiday stories that I'm sure you'll enjoy. The series kicks off with a free prequel novella, CHRISTMAS SISTERS, where you'll get a chance to meet the characters during their first Christmas together.

You won't want to miss THE WISHING TREE SERIES, set in Vermont. This series centers on a famed tree in the middle of the quaint town that is thought to grant wishes to those who tie them on her branches.

FROM THE AUTHOR

Readers love this series and always comment how they are full of hope, which we all need more of right now.

I'd love to send you my exclusive interview with the canine companions in my Hometown Harbor Series as a thank-you for joining my exclusive group of readers. You can sign up www.tammylgrace.com by clicking this link: https://wp.me/P9umIy-e

MORE FROM TAMMY L. GRACE

COOPER HARRINGTON DETECTIVE NOVELS

Killer Music

Deadly Connection

Dead Wrong

Cold Killer

HOMETOWN HARBOR SERIES

Hometown Harbor: The Beginning (Prequel Novella)

Finding Home

Home Blooms

A Promise of Home

Pieces of Home

Finally Home

Forever Home

CHRISTMAS STORIES

A Season for Hope: Christmas in Silver Falls Book 1

The Magic of the Season: Christmas in Silver Falls Book 2

Christmas in Snow Valley: A Hometown Christmas Book 1

One Unforgettable Christmas: A Hometown Christmas Book 2

Christmas Wishes: Souls Sisters at Cedar Mountain Lodge

Christmas Surprises: Soul Sisters at Cedar Mountain Lodge

Christmas Shelter: Soul Sisters at Cedar Mountain Lodge

GLASS BEACH COTTAGE SERIES

Beach Haven

Moonlight Beach

Beach Dreams

WRITING AS CASEY WILSON

A Dog's Hope

A Dog's Chance

WISHING TREE SERIES

The Wishing Tree

Wish Again

Overdue Wishes

SISTERS OF THE HEART SERIES

Greetings from Lavender Valley

Remember to subscribe to Tammy's exclusive group of readers for your gift, only available to readers on her mailing list. **Sign up at www.tammylgrace.com. Follow this link to subscribe at https://wp.me/P9umIy-e** and you'll receive the exclusive interview she did with all the canine characters in her Hometown Harbor Series.

Follow Tammy on Facebook by liking her page. You may also follow Tammy on her pages on book retailers or at BookBub by clicking on the follow button.

ABOUT THE AUTHOR

Tammy L. Grace is the *USA Today* bestselling and award-winning author of the Cooper Harrington Detective Novels, the bestselling Hometown Harbor Series, and the Glass Beach Cottage Series, along with several sweet Christmas novellas. Tammy also writes under the pen name of Casey Wilson for Bookouture and Grand Central. You'll find Tammy online at www.tammylgrace.com where you can join her mailing list and be part of her exclusive group of readers. Connect with Tammy on Facebook at www.facebook.com/tammylgrace.books or Instagram at @authortammylgrace.

- facebook.com/tammylgrace.books
- twitter.com/TammyLGrace
- instagram.com/authortammylgrace
- bookbub.com/authors/tammy-l-grace
- goodreads.com/tammylgrace

Made in the USA
Monee, IL
14 October 2024